For Us...

By LEW ANDERSON

THE LORIAN STONES TRILOGY

Book One: *Tombs of Dross*

Book Two: *Battles Grim*

Book Three: *Pillars and Power*

———————————

THE LORIAN CHRONICLES

Horse Boy

———————————

Misty Grey

Yodin the Rescuer

For Us

LEW ANDERSON

A FARM BOY, A PERSIAN PRINCESS, AN ISLAND

For Us...

TREESTONE BOOKS

Treestone Books

Boise

Publisher's Note: This novel is a work of fiction. Names, characters, places, and incidents are either products of the author's imagination or used fictitiously. All characters are fiction, and any similarity to people living or dead is purely coincidental.

ISBN 978-1-955486-09-5

*To my brother Paul who always loves a good story
And my friend Brad whose ceaseless encouragement
has been much appreciated*

SHIPWRECK

1

THE WHOLE SHIP SHUDDERED, walls and panels trembling as when death comes unannounced. A screaming shrill of metal, torn and twisted, screeched through the cabin walls. Objects rattled, crashing to the floor.

Jake tumbled from his bunk, listening in the darkness as an eerie silence followed. Then a thunderous roar shook the tiny cabin. Like some cornered creature, the room shivered, quaking and quivering, then it groaned—a forlorn cry for mercy.

Pulling on cargo shorts and a t-shirt, Jake paused to listen once more. A growing tumult of screams and shouts filled the hall outside his door. Their cries and running footsteps told of the chaotic clamoring, a hundred terrified passengers fighting through the crowded hall.

The floor began to slant, not much, but enough to send its foreboding message. Emergency lights flickered as if struggling to shed their light onto the rising chaos.

The lean young man poked his head warily out the cabin door. A passing arm whacked his ear. The narrow hall had already become a packed mass of confusion—screaming women and bossy men, pushing and shoving, some going one way, some the other, all calling for answers.

With a loud, agonizing groan the ship listed further, the floor now sloping at a frightening angle.

How can it be sinking? Jake thought with heart racing.

A small cruise ship, just under 400 passengers, it was a marvel of modern engineering, a floating cruiser of plush luxury and exquisite delight. *These ships don't sink, do they?*

A heavy-set man stumbled into his doorway, knocking Jake back into his room. The panic in the jammed hall had risen to a crescendo of shrieks and pleading cries.

These were economy cabins, the furthest from the top. The screams increased as the pack pushed for the stairs. Jake took a few deep breaths, grabbed his passport and wallet, then wedged his way into the hall.

An inch of water sloshed beneath the shuffling bare feet. A shadow of acrid smoke gently swirled above.

The yelling and screaming filled the hall like a fog, clouding all function of rational thought.

For a moment Jake just stood, banged and bumped as middle-aged overweight tourists fought each other for the stairs. The ship groaned again, leaning even more. This time the mass stumbled backward, arms flailing as bodies hit the floor.

A young blond, probably a college girl, went down in the rising water, her arms and legs pinned by frantic feet, feet driven by thoughts void of anything but survival. Jake pushed his way through and pulled her up.

"You okay?"

"What's happening?" she muttered, eyes roving wildly. Dressed only in a soft-pink top and shorts, she, like most, had jumped from her bed and into the hall.

"Not sure," Jake said, "but we've got to get out. Follow me."

He tried to push his way through, pulling the girl behind, but the ship kept listing. When they finally reached the steps, a steady flow of water cascaded over feet that did not move. The stairway had become a tangled mass of piled bodies pulling at each other, clamoring and clinging, slipping on the skin of those that lined the steps, skin fresh from cozy beds and bunks, now cast onto a sea-soaked floor of doom.

Fear struck hard as death loomed, its dark shadow whispering through the terrified crowd, its rapacious eye on those struggling to climb the crowded steps.

The floor moved again, sloping the hallway further,

sending screams to a mind-numbing siren of tortured souls on the brink of death.

"Back to my cabin!" Jake shouted, leading the girl away from the stairs. But now the surge had become a solid wall, multiple parts merged into one, a blockade of entrapment.

Jake smashed through a door, forcing his way into an empty cabin. He peered out the porthole, seeing only the blackness of the South Pacific sea. He eyed the girl standing beside him, her young frame trembling. A bleach-blond with nice eyes and lovely features.

Wish we'd met before all this.

A scraping sound came from far down the ship's stern. Jake tensed as it grew near. A horrid shrill of metal tearing metal, great objects of force and mass warring till the weaker surrenders, till the inferior yields.

Bolting backward, Jake pulled the girl away from the porthole just as metal tore through the cabin wall, shredding the side of the ship with deafening screeches. The two stumbled backward, both falling.

When Jake sat up, waves splashed below, droplets blowing inside the once warm cabin. The girl shrieked as the floor tilted toward the waves. The structure had buckled, opening the belly of the vessel. Jake knew all would be over in minutes.

"We have to jump!" he said, peering through the gap. "Swim clear before it rolls." He tugged for the girl to follow. She stood locked stiff, eyes wild. "Come on!" he shouted, tugging her arm. But nothing could break the stare of dread, the blanched look of death seizing her soul.

The jagged tear in the ship was just enough to crawl through, but the metal and wall panels had ripped like rows of teeth awaiting their victims. He flung a blanket over the metal and pulled once more at the girl. She jerked away, eyes wide.

"We can't stay!" he called. "We have to swim!" She slunk back, clinging to the door, her head shaking as her pale lips muttered. The ship jolted, then moaned like when death takes a weary body.

Jake pulled, but she fought, polished nails clawing and scratching. He looked for another blanket, thinking to roll her tight and toss her out, but then she was gone, squeezing back into the hallway of doom. The ship lunged to port side, sending Jake toppling toward the metal jaws, their ragged teeth gleaming. He shook his head, cursing as he carefully squeezed through the jagged gap.

"She'll never make it," he said, then dropped twenty feet into the black waters below.

THE WINE CASK

2

HE SWAM A FRENZIED STROKE, kicking hard, convinced the ship would list completely, roll and pull him down. He thrashed through the slow rolling waves as screams washed over the black waters, waters that reflected the lights of a hundred cabins, the glory and splendor of the luxury vessel whose innards now fanned out as the torn belly spewed the contents of a thousand objects, items of safety and comfort, of pleasure and leisure, all floating and bobbing on the waves that rolled casually on, unconcerned for the plight of those once aboard.

Jake rammed into something large, giving a hollow thud of heavy plastic bumping human head. A very large, yellow barrel rose with the swell. He looked back, surprised at how far he'd swum. The ship leaned so far now, three-fourths of the stern lay submerged, its lights flickering beneath the waves. Bodies hit the water from multiple angles, their final screams drifting out over the dark waters.

He tried to grasp the barrel, to find a handhold, a rope, or clasp. Completely round with a belly wider than the ends, it rocked and spun as he worked his way around. The top or end of the cask had a large cap set off center, at least two feet wide with indents for spinning it on and off.

"What the heck is this?" He fought to hold the cap, digging his fingers into the underside. The oversized barrel had to be empty for it sat high above the surge, bobbing easily as he hung, panting to catch his breath.

The cap turned, spinning just a bit, enough to plant a thought.

The ship, that now lay ever closer to its watery grave, had left Funafuti, Tuvalu, three days ago on its way to Vanuatu. But they were midway, meaning any rescue was at least a day or two out.

"Unless a ship is nearby." *But all these people in the water.*

A sharp fear rose. These waters had sharks, the likes of which, when coming upon such a feast, somehow spread the word with rapid effectiveness.

Jake had read of ships going down during wars, ships that lost hundreds to the sharks before rescue arrived.

A frightening chill shook him as he looked back toward the small cruise ship. He looked for lifeboats, seeing only jumpers, plunging as flames now poured from the sinking vessel.

He trembled as he worked the cover, gripping with both hands, pulling himself up out of the waves as he turned. Finally, it spun free, opening a portal into a huge empty barrel. A sweet fragrance of fruity wine billowed from the cask.

He felt the inside of the lid, finding small indents, enough to grip and hold.

If I could climb in... screw this lid back on... but not too tight...

"Feet first," he told himself but struggled for some time trying to enter without letting water rush in. Screams and cries continued to roll over the waves, growing fainter and fewer as he tread water, clinging to the open portal.

Flotsam fanned out beneath the dimming lights of the ship, rising like a blanket of trash upon the dark sea. A plastic mug floated by, white with red lettering.

Jake stretched, reluctant to release the giant barrel. "I need that mug!" He pushed away from the barrel and swam, the lid in one hand, grabbing for the cup with the other. Just as he turned to swim back to the wine cask, a cry drifted over the darkness, a soft cry for help, the cry of a young woman.

Using the cover he pushed upward to look out over the waves. Nothing. He paused to listen. Only the drifting cries now carried by the wind.

With cup in one hand, the large lid in the other, he swam hard back to the bobbing barrel, spurred by the dreadful thought of losing it, of losing his only hope. Just as he tossed the plastic mug inside, the soft cry came once more.

He spun to face the sound, straining to see with salted eyes, searching for a head above the waves. Then it came again, a muffled cry, a desperate plea.

A black silhouette of an outstretched arm suddenly rose, caught by the firelight of the sinking ship. Just out of its reach, a life jacket bobbed in the waves.

"Can you swim?" Jake called to the hand but saw it drop with a splash, the gargled reply giving answer. Groaning he tugged at the barrel, kicking toward the cry. Without any way of knowing distance, he tried to focus on the spot, but waves rose and fell, jerking at his precious barrel, pushing him this way and that.

He brushed a limb, smooth skin against his arm, hair wrapping about his wrist. A young woman rose as he pulled. He called for her to answer, struggling to lift her head.

Sputtering and gasping, her face broke the surface, hair swirling over eyes and mouth.

"Grab this!" Jake pulled her arm to the cask hole, handing her the large lid. Her whole frame trembled as he held her up.

Lightening flashed from a dark band rising over the sinking ship. Drops came in heavy thumps, drumming the large barrel as if searching for some savage rhythm.

"Climb in," Jake said, struggling to hold the barrel

steady. "Feet first. Careful, the sides are rough." But the young woman hesitated, sputtering a host of unknown words.

"Sharks," Jake said. "We need to get inside. I'll help you."

What followed was short of disastrous comedy. As Jake tried to lift her legs, the young woman's head went under. As her head went under, legs came out. The rain fell heavier, pounding the drum with rhythmic beats of warlike tempo, calling for the blackness, awakening the night.

After too many minutes of vain attempts, Jake explained he would crawl in first and pull her in.

With no less frustration, he squeezed his shoulders through, leaving some skin at the opening's rim. The challenge was to keep from rolling inside the barrel as waves grew with the building storm. The distant rumblings drowned out the last of the piteous cries, cooler air now rolling over the waves, blown in by the rising wind.

"Take my hand," he said, reaching out the portal. "It's going to hurt a bit."

With painful cries of protest, of banged shins and scraped thighs, the slender arms and legs of a frightened young woman finally tangled with those of a tawny young man inside a large plastic barrel drifting somewhere along the South Pacific Rim.

It took some time to undo themselves, to balance the stout barrel, to limit the banging heads and craned limbs, realizing in the process that they had lost the lid. With their weight together at the bottom, the cask bobbed upright, but the driving rain had no trouble finding the two-foot opening overhead.

It was black inside, so Jake had no idea with whose limbs he sat entangled, other than her accent sounded Middle Eastern.

"Are you hurt?" he asked, bracing himself against the sides, the waves now playing hard with this new toy.

Only panting breaths and sniffling whimpers came in reply.

Hope she doesn't get seasick, Jake thought, as a wave lifted them high, then let them plummet. His stomach lurched with sudden nausea. *Oh, boy. Hope I don't get sick.*

When a lull came, Jake sighed, trying to take in the last hour. What had taken out the ship? He could still see the blond with wild eyes staring, the screech of metal ripping through the ship, the explosion, the jammed bodies in the hall of doom. And now crammed in a three-by-four-foot wine cask with a young woman who may not even speak English.

In their awkward fumbling to crawl inside, he knew she wore little for clothing, had incredibly soft skin, was slender yet shapely, and her long, thick hair seemed bent on catching and tangling everywhere.

He sighed again. "A dream," he muttered. "Those kind you're so relieved when you finally wake up."

The girl gave a stuttering sob, whole body shivering.

FISH IN A BARREL

3

SOMEHOW THEY ENDURED with agonizing cramps, cries of mercy, and bumps from sharks or whatever swims about banging large casks floating an endless ocean with rain-filled skies.

Jake tried to speak words of encouragement, of rescue, that it wouldn't be long, and search parties were already picking people up, but his soul didn't believe a word of it.

Something's off, he mused. *How had it sunk so fast?*

The girl coughed, suppressing a heave.

"Hang in there," he said, as the foot of water inside

sloshed about. "I'll bail this water when the waves let up."

He longed to stand and check things out, but the waves now rocked them hard. After an hour of hearing only rain and their own limbs banging the sides, a host of fears began to stir.

Where is the rescue? he wondered in frustration, fully expecting to hear helicopters or foghorns, anything that told of rescue.

Could take hours, he reproached himself. *Days even.* "No, there must be a ship nearby," he muttered.

But nothing came, only the rain's steady beat against the cask as the waves lifted and tossed the barrel side to side.

He glanced up. "If we had the lid," he said, "could tip this thing on its side… give us more room, be more stable… maybe."

The girl sniffled like a scolded child.

"No," he said quickly, "not blaming, just thinking. We can't sit crunched like this much more."

Having swum so hard in the waves, to now sit with legs crammed tight, was already pushing him toward madness. With no way to stretch, he could only rub his muscles, finding little relief.

The girl sat with legs drawn tight to her chest, trying desperately to sit sideways as she shivered, hunched in a tight ball.

His legs were to each side, his knees at her shoulders, bare feet wrapped around behind her back. Beyond awkward, and seriously uncomfortable, he wondered if he'd made the right choice.

Would work for one, he argued. But then recalled her weak arm reaching for help, her sputtering cry. *Should've put her in the life jacket. Waited with her.* He shook his head. *Waited till the sharks came?*

Struggling to brace himself, he had one arm extended above her head, the other clutching the rim above. But the storm had come to play and it tossed them every which way.

He'd apologize each time he bumped her hard, or fought to work out a cramp. Her tense groans clearly conveyed she found this whole affair worse than death, even if by shark.

Then her leg cramped. Crying out, she kicked Jake in the groin as she tried to work it out. Clutching her knotted calf, she uttered unknown words. Pleas or curses, he couldn't tell.

He offered a hand but got a firm slap. So, he sat silent, his groin aching in the plastic darkness as she muttered, rubbing her calf.

After an eternal night of nausea, pain, and crippling stiffness, the sea had calmed, the cask now rocking gently. In the hint of a yellowish glow, Jake sat pondering, careful not to move.

Though sore in every joint, he studied the sleeping maiden entrapped with him. She slept with cheek upon her shoulder, arms limp at her sides. Her desperate struggle to keep from touching him had long since failed, for her legs, like his, filled every space the cask offered.

As the glow brightened, he studied the weary face before him. Long hair hung loose, veiling most of her features. She moaned and twitched now and then, followed by a shiver.

Once again he questioned his judgment. *Should've put her in the life jacket. Found a boat or something, anything other than this… this plastic tomb of aching misery.*

She jerked, knocking him hard, but didn't wake. When her head flopped to the other shoulder, Jake gasped.

Oh, my God! No way!

Mouth hanging, Jake stared wide-eyed, his head shaking in disbelief. "Can't be. No way."

The first day into their cruise, he had been taking photos from a balcony when an entourage of dark suits and flowing head-wraps had come onto a private deck. Amid the suits walked a slender woman, early twenties if that, her long dark hair, thick and wavy, lifting freely in the sea breeze. She toyed with the wind, her hair and silks flowing gently about.

For a time, she stood at the rail, staring out over the waves. She turned, expecting to see no one outside her entourage, and to be seen by no outsider, for her customary veil lay loose about her long, bejeweled neck.

And that's when their eyes met—three seconds, maybe, but it was enough. She looked quickly away and he knew he'd better do the same. Three big suits with dark glasses turned his way.

With a nod, he was gone. But those three seconds… He had been instantly convinced she was the most beautiful and stunningly gorgeous woman he had ever seen in his entire life.

She carried such poise and grace with her features and form, and even with all the silk trappings, he could see her figure was no trifling of the gods. From head to toe, this girl personified mind-numbing beauty reserved only for those of legends and lore.

Later that day, he'd learned she was the daughter of Fariborz Rahbar, a sheik or something, a guy with more money and wives than any man should have. For the next three days he tried to reach that balcony again but always found the door firmly bolted with a warning.

He now stared at the young woman entangled so close, her neck craned. *No, can't be,* he argued. *She'd have been whisked away by chopper, or set in a lifeboat. Probably on a beach in Tuvalu by now.* He shook his head, straining to see more in the dim yellowish glow. "No, Jake," he whispered, "you're still sleeping… dreaming stupid dreams."

But then she twitched, her large dark eyes opening wide with alarm. Like a trapped animal, she stared at the young man just inches away, then quickly glanced about the glowing barrel.

Dark fear filled her face as she peered down, immediately covering herself. Her skimpy silk top and matching peach-colored shorts did little for modesty. She scowled, her eyes burning with bitter rage.

But Jake remained stuck in his bewildered stare.

She huffed, giving the sternest glare a woman can muster. Snapping out of his stupor, Jake gave a respectful nod and looked away, even though there was simply no other place to look.

Breathing fast through her nose, she glanced about, as if searching for some escape. For a moment, Jake thought she would bolt up and try climbing out, but she kept her arms wrapped tight about her long legs which were pulled snug to her chest.

With awkward bumps and elbows in her face, Jake took off his *Big Sky Montana* t-shirt and looking away, held it out. She exhaled in disgust, the idea utterly inconceivable. He then looked her in the eyes, offering the shirt one last time.

For a tense moment, she held his gaze, finally taking the worn damp t-shirt using only thumb and finger.

Jake ceremonially closed his eyes and waited.

He had to fight back a smirk as she didn't move, still breathing hard through her nose. Then some strange, but nasty-sounding words got muttered as she struggled to don the rugged t-shirt.

When she finished, Jake nodded approvingly and introduced himself.

"Jake… from Montana… Bozeman."

She gave no reply other than more hot breath through flared nostrils.

"Tell me you're not the sheik's daughter," he said plainly. "That it wasn't you that day… on the deck?"

As if bitten, she gasped, then quickly looked away.

"Oh, God," Jake groaned, shaking his head. "This is bad." Seeing she understood English, he asked, "How'd you end up in the water? Is your father… okay? Does he know what happened to you? And those guys… your bodyguards?"

Her face tensed, pondering these same things, but still offered no exchange, her full lips pressed tight.

Over a foot of water sloshed with the swaying of the barrel, soaking their butts and feet. Jake yearned to start bailing, but it would be awkward.

"Any idea what happened?" he asked. "Was some kind of explosion."

She continued to look away, a shadow of angst darkening her face.

"I need to bail this water," he said, trying to speak gently, as if to a frightened child. "It's going to be awkward. But if we can dry things out…"

She turned to study him for a bit, then gave a slight nod—a first in communication.

Minor awkwardness followed, trying to bring the cup up without bonking or spilling as it went up and down. Then his leg cramped and he had to stand.

Forcing his shoulders through the porthole into the morning's light, he breathed deep, drawing his toes upward to stretch his calf.

Stern mutterings came from below. *Probably cursing me to the deepest hell about now,* he mused with a chuckle. But being just over six feet, he had to stretch his limbs. He glanced down to see her pressed back, hands covering her face.

He scanned the horizon, careful not to tip the barrel. The cask rode halfway in the waves, bobbling like a buoy. He turned about, fully expecting to see the ship where it had been last night.

But the sea lay bare, yielding only the sun's reddish reflection, its shimmering glow announcing the new day. All evidence of the ship had vanished, nothing but waves and endless sky. He squinted, looking long into the empty horizon.

"There's got to be something… come on! A ship would have passed by, got the message, called it in."

A swell of weary despair washed over him. Again he turned about, scanning the vast horizon of nothing.

When he wriggled back into the cask, bumping her more than once, she gave only minimal protest. Her eyes followed him as he slunk back down, his face revealing their plight.

At first, he couldn't face her, chiding himself harshly. *What was I thinking? Drag the sheik's daughter into an oversized barrel where no one can see us… hidden from rescue. Good lord, that was brilliant.*

He felt her eyes on him and looked up. She had an innate intelligence as she studied his face. Then she spoke, her voice dry and rasping, her accent clearly Middle Eastern.

"Nothing?"

Jake sat silent, just staring at her lips.

"You see nothing?" she asked again.

He sighed. "I'm sorry."

In silence they sat, swaying with the waves, drifting

aimless in the open sea, a thousand miles from any-where, crammed together in a cask of yellow plastic, one dressed only in scanty silks, the other in worn-out cargo shorts. A guy from Montana and a princess of some-where, drifting without water, without direction, without food, and without space to move.

"At least…" the girl said, forcing a dry swallow, "we are safe from shark."

Only inches away, Jake searched her eyes, still mysti-fied by her presence. Then he gave a consenting nod. "Yeah… we are safe from the sharks."

ISLE OF SUNSET
4

AS A RED SUN ROSE, Jake worked at bailing water. The sea had calmed, but the cask grew warm, so, with no little calamity, Jake wriggled out and into the sea.

Alone inside, the girl was at first hesitant to stand and stretch, but Jake balanced the cask, and she stood with hands clutching the rim.

Holding the barrel as he tread water, he searched the sea in desperate earnest. *You fool,* he chided once again. *What have you done?*

The girl too searched as she stood, the rim just below her shoulders. Arms outside, she balanced herself, long hair drifting in the gentle wind like that day on the upper deck.

"See anything?" Jake asked, hoping her eyes were keener, but she only shook her head in slow disbelief.

When Jake crawled back inside, he had to again bail water, but this time his guest seemed less annoyed.

After a time, when the cask and their clothes were mostly dry, the girl cleared her throat, and lifting her chin, proudly declared.

"I am Misha Kamineh Parim Mehrak, daughter of the great Fariborz Rahbar, ruler of the lands of Lahar."

A bit startled, Jake nodded. She was indeed the girl with the entourage. "Jake Connor, ruler of my car and whatever else the bank doesn't own."

Though she fought it, a subtle smile tweaked her lips.

As the day grew warm, the girl slowly revealed more, granting glimpses into her life of luxury, but not of ease, as she readily made known.

Being only nineteen, she could never be allowed to speak to a young infidel like Jake, let alone be seen by him, especially in such a state. So to be alone with him, so close and dressed in things that would bring great shame even in her own bedroom, was unspeakable.

"So not even as pajamas?" Jake asked, careful not to sound judgmental.

"This…" She gestured toward the glowing barrel, then to the ragged t-shirt and silk top beneath, her gaze returning to Jake as if to say, 'and you.' "This…" she continued, wagging her head in bewilderment, "…is detestable sin beyond… beyond my English words."

"Well, if it helps, the t-shirt looks good on you." *Anything would look good on you,* he almost said.

She closed her eyes with a heavy sigh, sorrow again darkening her face.

"We'll get out of this," Jake said, struggling to believe his own words. "And… you're safe with me. I'm not that kind of… *infidel.*" He spoke sincerely. "Just really sorry I dragged you into this." He huffed a wry chuckle as he glanced about their yellow cell, recalling the comedic efforts to get her inside the rolling cask.

She studied him, looking long into his eyes, which they both knew was also 'forbidden.'

By noon, the sun had grown hot, but then the sky clouded. By late afternoon, the sea had settled, so Jake suggested they lean the barrel over, keeping the offset opening on the upward side, clear of any waves.

"I assure you, Misha of Lahar, my intentions are purely to get you back to your father as safe and as soon as possible. Nothing more."

Using the t-shirt to cover herself as much as possible, she consented. He offered his cargo shorts, but she quickly refused, to which he was silently thankful.

Lying side by side, Jake took care to keep his limbs as contained as possible, though contact was unavoidable, their bodies sliding together no matter what positions they tried.

Misha struggled to compose herself in such a compromising predicament, but appreciated the freedom to move, and most of all, straighten her legs.

For Jake, having already been struck by the beauty of this mystery girl, to now be in such close quarters, was more than a bit bewildering.

Just Fate and the cosmos toying with lives again, he pondered in jest. *A cosmic convergence that will only create a mess for both of us. Or maybe the stars and planets have drifted completely out of celestial alignment… or Fate and Love are contending… with no one left to monitor the feeble stumblings of mankind.* He softly chuckled, then sighed. *Or I'm having a most fantastical dream.*

Stay focused! he rebuked himself, as an image of them drifting for days without water, their bodies shrinking, faces gaunt, came in a disturbing flash.

May very well die in this stupid barrel! An urgency to do something filled his veins. *But what? Should have captured that rainwater at least. But how?*

That night they shivered, Jake once more blaming himself for their predicament, wishing he had some way to relieve her discomfort. Yet somehow they managed to snatch bouts of restless sleep.

The following day grew hot as the sun beat upon the bobbing cask. Though hungry, it was the heat and thirst that became unbearable, especially for the young woman accustomed to luxury.

Only by necessity did Misha climb out and spend some time in the water. Being a poor swimmer and still fearing sharks, she at first held tight to the rim.

But the sea was calm, so together they drifted in the gentle swell, clinging to the cask as they tread water, eyes always searching the vast, empty horizon.

"I'll stay out if you want to get some sleep," Jake offered, noticing the dark shadows beneath her light-brown eyes.

She shook her head. "So warm inside. The water feel nice."

Nothing had bumped their cask in a long time, and so they drifted with little fear. Misha rested her head on her hands as she clung to the barrel, her black hair swirling with the flow.

"Do you have any brothers," Jake asked, "that would come looking for you?" He feared her father had gone down with the ship.

Misha shook her head. "No. No brothers or sisters. Just me."

"Really?" Jake figured there would be a dozen or more. He almost asked the number of wives her father had but caught himself in time.

"The Rockies are beautiful," he said, changing the subject to Montana and his life in America. For this, she had many questions, which at times he found amusing, her perceptions stemming from Hollywood.

"You have woman?" Misha asked.

"A girlfriend? No."

"Why not?"

Before he'd realized, he told her about his fiancé running off with his best friend, and how he'd left the small town to work odd jobs on the islands, wandering from place to place, trying to forget his past and find purpose.

With fresh remorse, he told how the two had died just last month in an avalanche while backcountry skiing, almost a year to the day she had left him.

What had begun as a plan to simply distract the young princess from their desperate plight, had grown into a full-out session on the therapist's couch.

"I should have done more," Jake said ruefully. "Should have protected her from him."

Misha watched him, her brow knit. "Today is… all sovereign over yesterday," she said, struggling to express her thought. "Does not the road ahead… reign over that which is behind?" She paused, brow still knit. "Did I say this right?"

Jake slowly nodded in surprise. "Yes, all too right."

She smiled, but then looked pensive. "We must keep trust that Allah watches," she said, this time struggling to believe her own words.

"Yeah, not seeing any God up there right now," Jake replied sullenly. "If he is, he sure ain't watching."

Misha fell silent, her own heart pondering the hand of Allah, of fate and life, and now… a very possible agonizing death.

That evening of their second day adrift, Misha lay with her head and hands outside the barrel, staring into the sunset. Jake lay on his back, eyes drowsy, stomach sunken.

Tears moistened the girl's eyes as she gently used her hands to keep the opening toward the sunset. She seemed to be praying, her soft lips murmuring.

Then, lifting her head, she muttered something, paused a moment, and then… screamed.

Jake bolted, quickly pulling her inside. "What happened? Something bite you?"

"Look!" she said, pointing through the hatch. "Land! I see land!"

A faint rise on the horizon cast a long dull shadow as the sun edged near the sea. It was indeed land. But it was hours away and the sun was near set. Jake strained, searching for lights, hoping with all hope that it was occupied and not some remote little island without habitation.

He tried to observe their drift, hoping the current would take them near.

"Island?" he wondered aloud, "or a coast?"

"But no lights," Misha said softly.

Jake cursed the growing darkness, trying to find some way to set a course. Keeping his eye on the spot, he called for a star, for a moon, for anything to mark the sky.

"The moon will show us," Misha said rather calmly. "It will rise soon, we then see."

The moon did rise within the hour. Its glow on the open sea gave an enchanting display of wonder. As it climbed, its glow filling the night sky, they drifted closer to the 'Isle of Sunset,' as Misha called it.

When the moon was high, they passed near the land. It seemed to be an island maybe two miles from their bright yellow barrel. That they would pass completely by was also clear, so Jake climbed out and swam.

Misha watched. "I very much not like the water at night," she softly confessed. She had told him early on that she was not a good swimmer and really did not enjoy being in the sea.

Kicking hard, Jake pulled and pushed the barrel, watching the isle drift further and further to the left. After an hour or more, he clung exhausted to the open hatch.

"I'm sorry," he panted, "but we'll have… to swim it. I can't get us there… in time."

So out she crawled, and with one hand on his shoulder, she kicked, trailing as he swam in the desperation that only those who have tasted such hopeless despair, seeing life itself drifting by, can understand.

Cursing, yet crying out for God to prove himself, Jake pushed against the current, aiming for the moonlit mass of hope that sat so distant, so passive, too indolent to aid their dying souls.

Time fussed with the darkness as muscles cramped, eyes blurred, hope fading with every endless stroke. Misha more and more lost her grip, her strength gone from days without food and water.

Something happens in those times of forsaken souls. Fragile walls of life give way to the core of being, to the spirit that often lies hidden, reserved deep inside. That which matters most, which matters only, comes to the forefront. Life, that delicate, precious gift so easily taken, yet easily preserved when conditions are right, dangles in the balance. It floats just a breaststroke away, just a few more yards, calling your name, beckoning you to keep trying, to keep moving, to do anything other than give in.

Crying out, Misha jerked away, grabbing at her ankle. Then Jake jolted, as several sharp stings burned into his bare chest. Like an early alarm, it shook him from the endless swim. He looked up, seeing a mass of darkness high above them—the Isle of Sunset.

Again, Misha cried out, trying not to scream, but the pain came so quick, like bee stings that burned.

Jake paused, a sting to his thigh. He cursed, but his dry throat made no sound. Then the stings came from everywhere. They both cried out, Misha now screaming and kicking.

Seeing the island so close, Jake pulled her up onto his back.

"Hang on," he tried to say, kicking and swimming with the little that remained, the burning pain fueling his strength.

They rose and fell in the waves, his feet touching just a moment before rising high with the swell.

The moon leaned toward the west by the time they crawled up the beach, collapsing on the warm sand. Misha cried with agony, frantically rubbing her skin as the gentle surf rolled in behind them, crabs scurrying about in the wash of the moon's light.

FIRST NIGHT

5

PULSING RED BURNS tormented their bodies as they lay side-by-side on the warm sands of the Isle of Sunset.

"Don't rub them," Jake tried to say, but his voice had become a dry whisper. "Try…to remove… the stingers."

Despite all the agony, Jake sighed with deep relief, rich gratitude filling his heart. Whether on a small island or a coast, he cared little—it was land.

Misha sobbed, still rubbing the stings, trying not to openly bawl. In all her life, she had never experienced such pain.

Jake thought of how some people actually pee on jellyfish stings, the acidic urine neutralizing the alkaline sting. In all his pain and exhaustion he chuckled, picturing her response to such a suggestion.

Couldn't anyway, even to save my life.

Thirst had grown into a nagging pain. They were severely dehydrated, feeling it everywhere.

In the dim light, Jake tried to pick the stinging bits left by the nasty creatures. Some burned hot, but to just lie there in pain, so hungry and thirsty, seemed pointless. The moon lit the isle enough to navigate, so after a time, Jake urged Misha to her feet.

"We need water," he tried to say.

She rose, gritting her teeth, making great effort to suppress the cries of agony, to stately endure the tormenting of her tender skin.

Not something I'd expect from a sheik's princess, Jake marveled. He wished he could pee, if it would actually help. "Vinegar," he muttered, "need vinegar."

For a moment they stood together looking up at the looming blackness before them. Jake glanced back over the sea, the surf glowing in the moonlight.

"Sorry for all that," he said. "But we're on land... out of that... crazy barrel."

She gave no reply, her teeth still clenched, trying hard to suppress the sniffles, and outbursts of pain.

Jake cursed, wishing he had some way to help her. His own skin burned everywhere, throbbing pains that came in tormenting waves.

"So sorry," he said again. "Can you walk?"

By moonlight they moved cautiously over dried fronds, weaving through scattered palms that lined the beach. Columns of dark rock rose among the trees, leading toward a cliff that towered high over the beach, its face looming like a watchman, steady at his post.

A faint, eerie howl drifted through the trees. Jake stopped. Misha turned to run back.

"Stay with me," he said, grabbing her hand. They stood listening, hand-in-hand, slowly turning about to find the source. But like all sounds that come in the night, they seem to know when their victims are listening. Nothing more came, so on they walked, following the paths of moonlight through the thickening forest of palms, the wind rustling gently over all that caught its caress.

Again the moaning howl came, louder this time—a low, hollow breathing, softly dissipating as they stopped to listen. Again they waited with Misha pulling back toward the beach, although holding Jake's hand tighter with each step.

"I think it's the wind," Jake whispered. "Could be a cave or something." Then he stopped, tilting his head. "Is that water?"

He followed the steady sound of running water, ignoring the eerie moans that came and went, until a sudden shriek shot through the night.

Misha screamed, jerking free to run back through the trees, tripping over fronds, her frightened cries echoing with the surf.

Jake called out as he ran behind, trying to follow the

erratic path, ducking and dodging, till they both stood on the beach panting in the moonlight.

"Why you take me there?" she spouted, stamping her feet. "Oh, I hurt. All over I hurt so bad."

"I know. I'm sorry," he said, trying to calm her. "Was just a monkey or something, maybe a bird."

She hopped about, arms waving as she broke into a hard sob.

Jake watched, frustrated. "We can stay out here for the night," he said, wishing he could help her somehow. *Help myself, for that matter.*

For a time she paced about, shaking her arms and crying. When Jake suggested they find a place to sleep near the trees, she just shook her head.

When the burning eased, she stood facing the waves, her sniffles carried off by the evening wind.

Jake spread some grass beneath a tree near the surf, making another for himself a good ten feet away.

He stretched out, the stings still annoying, his throat painful with thirst. He longed to search out the sound of water, but the present mental state of his royal princess would keep them near the waves, at least for the night.

He watched her standing by the surf, long hair lifting in the gentle wind. His t-shirt hung just below her shorts, but left her long, slender legs to glimmer in the moonlight. With arms folded, she turned to see him watching. He gestured toward the grass bedding.

Taking one last look, she peered out over the dark waters, then made her way up the sand to where Jake had laid out the grass.

She stood waiting for something. After a moment, Jake rolled the other way, and soon her grass bedding crinkled. Soft sniffles came and went as the moon moved over the hills following the sun to end another day.

QUENCHING A THIRST
6

WHEN JAKE AWOKE, the sun shone hot upon his feet. With lips cracked and bleeding, he tried to swallow the dryness. He sat up and looked about the beach.

Misha was gone. He rubbed his stubble and salt-crusted hair, stretched sore muscles, and rejoiced the painful stings had passed. Scanning the sand and rock, he rose and followed the footprints meandering along the surf, seeing where she stopped here and there, entered the waves, and then disappeared beneath a cliff.

When he rounded a boulder, he stopped, surprised to see Misha holding a small rock above her head, poised over a cornered crab the size of a silver dollar. She flung the rock, missing the crab, which scurried straight toward her feet making her jump and scream.

Jake laughed.

Misha spun, her face livid. "How you dare laugh, infidel! You never to laugh at me, never!" She stormed off further down the beach.

"Well, good morning to you too," he said, wagging his head. He turned back to search for the water, grumbling things that people say when they're hungry and thirsty, sore and weary, scorned by *'a rich brat who wouldn't last a day in the real world.'*

With every step, he grumbled on, but every word met resistance. She was different—more than just beautiful, and neither was she a simple rich snob. *Endured hell... without complaining. Endured me... for that matter.* No, she was different from any girl he had ever known.

He found the source of the water sounds, a trickling seep dripping high up on a cliff, splashing over rocks that put it back into the air from which it came. He would have to climb to drink.

The volcanic rock, sharp and black, gave tiny holes that made climbing easy, though painful. Never had water tasted so good, so cool, so fresh and sweet. After only two drinks he felt conviction.

But how would she climb? he pondered. *How could I carry it down?*

He drank till his stomach hurt, finding it hard to leave, always taking one last drink. Finally, he climbed down and went in search of Misha.

He called for her as he hobble-jogged back down the beach, searching for something in which to hold water.

For some time he followed her tiny prints, climbing over rocks and through palm-covered patches, traversing ledges that seemed far too precarious for one such as Misha to be walking.

Must be really mad, he thought.

The sun grew hot, his belly growled. Awakened by the water, his hunger grew intense. He grumbled again at the 'dumb chick' for wandering so far from the water. He crossed a rock outcropping that extended far into the surf and suddenly stopped.

There, face down on the sand, lay Misha, Princess of Lahar.

Cradling the comatose girl in his arms, he trekked back over the arduous path she had taken. Straining beneath the heat, he hastened on, admiring and fearing for the gentle beauty limp over his arms. Stopping briefly to rest and look for water, he cursed himself for letting her be alone, for saying what he had, for not being more patient.

He carried her all the way to the water source, finding no place to drink other than the high cliff. Finally he climbed, filling his mouth with water, climbing back down to press his lips to hers, praying she wouldn't choke.

She awoke with a start, her eyes wide at seeing his face so close. A swift arm clobbered Jake on the ear. The water spewed from his mouth as he tumbled to the side, stunned by the sudden blow.

Misha tried to stand but could not, her legs refusing to move. She yelled something in her native tongue and tried to fling sand into the eyes of her attacker. Jake crawled away, rubbing his ringing ear.

"You need water," he said, sitting a good distance away. "You walked too far in the sun." He waited as she felt the tiny drops spattering from above. She saw the water he had spewed from his mouth, and studied the look on his face.

This man Jake was different, not like any man she had ever known.

"I couldn't carry you up," he said, still winded. "Was the only way I could…" He trailed off, working to catch his breath. "Maybe… if you hold on, I can carry you up… I hope."

He watched her intently studying him. "You need water, Misha. You're seriously dehydrated."

Suddenly her head went woozy and her eyes rolled backward. She slumped, trying to keep an eye on the man called Jake. His voice, now distant, said something about carrying her up, for her to hold on. Then all went dark.

Jake tried to hoist her up and carry her to the water, but it proved impossible. It would be hard with her awake. So up he went, filling his mouth, determined to make her drink this time.

When he again pressed his lips to hers, squeezing her cheeks, he fully expected the same response but would keep his grip until she drank.

This time her lips opened slowly, as did her eyes and

without a struggle, she swallowed. Slowly she wiped her mouth, staring hard into his eyes.

He helped her stand, telling her to hold tight, and together they rose to the trickling water up on the cliff. With enough room to sit, they stared out over the trees and beach below, sipping and drinking as the sun rose higher.

After another long look at this one called Jake, Misha gave a very subtle nod.

"I thank you," she said in her soft, accented voice.

Surprised, Jake acknowledged, then looked away, an intense warmth rushing his heart and face. Everything he'd endured to this moment, even the darn jellyfish, seemed trivial to the sensation now pulsing.

From that moment on, his life would never be the same. Deep inside he vowed. Never again would she leave his sight, nor go thirsty, nor hungry, nor feel threatened.

Never again! He'd found his purpose, his sole reason for being. His thirsting soul had finally found its life-giving spring.

Jake Connor will be the man to bring this jewel of Persia back to her father, to present his missing treasure, unharmed, well fed, and safe from any who seek ill will.

FOOD

7

FOR SOME TIME THEY SAT, enjoying the water and wind, the view of the sea and rocky shores. Jake heard Misha's stomach growl. Like his belly, hers too had been awakened. They would need to find food, which may also mean fire.

Jake was a country boy, raised on a small farm, spending summers shooting rabbits and squirrels, using everything from slingshots to shotguns. He had killed and dressed big game at thirteen and was good with a bow.

He had read some about wilderness survival and starting a fire from scratch, but never actually tried, other than with magnesium and flint. He knew what to do, but doing is often far more difficult than knowing.

It seemed much harder climbing down, his strength giving way just feet from the bottom. They landed with a rather painful thump on the grassy sand. Misha said nothing as she brushed her bronze-colored legs and arms, red welts dotting her skin.

They thought to search the beaches and rocky crags for food, remembering the crab incident, for which Jake genuinely apologized.

With their minds on food, the hunger increased all the more, making patient searches all the harder. Jake found a pool where creatures scurried with the surge, dashing in every direction with his attempts at capture.

They would need help.

Having not yet seen any sign of human life, either in footprints, garbage, smoke, boats, or previous habitation, Jake concluded they were on a small island far from any land with human activity. Being only days at sea they could not be far from the shipping lanes, but the storm had come with strong winds that first night.

None of that mattered now, as there was but one thing on their minds—food.

The coconuts were either green in the trees or rotten on the ground. Something like bananas grew high in several trees, but their height and green color waned to beckon his interest. He did not wish to venture far from the water source so they made their way north, the opposite way Misha had gone that morning.

When two hours had passed with absolutely nothing

offering potential food, his heart began to falter. He stopped to rest, sitting on a rocky ridge that ran from the cliff behind to the surf rolling ever so steadily onto the sand and rocks.

Misha sat beside him, a little less conscious of her flimsy attire. A budding trust was taking root. This young man had shown himself to have only noble intentions, so unlike most men she had met.

It was a new and radical thought for her, warming her insides as she sat, clothed in his ragged t-shirt. Her hair, rich black through ages of Persian blood, was now stiff and dull, saturated with salt and sand.

This feeling of trust was new, exciting even. Every rule etched on her heart was being broken, but not of her choosing, not of rebellion against the ways of her father—no, it was unavoidable. They were simply trying to survive. Were she to find proper clothing, it would be with joy to cover herself in modesty, unlike those western women lacking even the simplest of morals.

Still, a warmth stirred. How could she find this exciting? Her stomach growled. She bit her lip, contemplating her next words.

"I believe in you, Yacov. I believe you will find food… for us." A subtle joy touched her soul. She liked the sound of those words, 'for us.'

Her heart quickened. She was no longer under her father's strict eye, no longer surrounded by the bodyguards in suits and dark glasses. She was alone with a handsome blond infidel on an island she named 'Sunset,' dressed in pajamas of which her father would never approve, wearing a t-shirt that would not even be allowed for the great hounds to shred. The joy came again, tickling her hungry belly.

"I'm free," she said, not intending to speak.

"What?" Jake asked.

Misha quickly shook her head, lips pressed tight. But then she turned away and smiled. *I'm free!*

Encouraged by her words, Jake rose, repeating the gentle sounds within. *I believe in you, Yacov.* As if she had breathed fresh life into his soul, he found new strength. No matter how many days they might be held captive on this desolate land, he would cherish those words like food for his soul. No matter what trials this island held for them, no matter how bent Fate seemed on destroying its two young victims, Jake would persevere.

I believe in you, Yacov.

When he climbed the ridge and stood, he almost buckled with delight. On the beach below, wallowing up an inlet of sand, crawled a tortoise, a sea tortoise the size of his mother's largest turkey roaster. With great excitement, he motioned for Misha to come quietly. They stood watching it work its way inland, laboring every foot.

"I need a knife," Jake said, wondering how to dress such an animal. He grabbed a rock to strike its head. Misha turned away, going back down, not wishing to see that which must be done.

It was a long time before Jake came back. He explained how the rock proved useless, the creature retracting into its shell, and how he then tried to suffocate the critter but didn't know such an animal could hold its breath indefinitely, and....

Misha grimaced.

"But I do need a knife," he said, crawling back over the ridge. "Something sharp. See what you can find… please."

She gave a slight smile and went toward the water's edge. Jake watched with a sigh.

Like some divine goddess, he mused, *sent to test… or torment, the hearts of men.* If he hadn't felt so miserably hungry and sore, this whole affair could be rather interesting, maybe even fun.

She glanced back and he quickly looked away, climbing hurriedly over the rocks.

Misha smiled, nurturing the flutter that warmed her heart.

A GOOD MAN

8

MISHA HAD FOUND SOME SHELLS and a sharp pointed stone. It was almost evening when Jake cried out with joy as tiny flames consumed the coconut fibers and shredded palm fronds. He had worked long shaping the tools for making his ember, which had created flame.

"The miracle of fire," he said softly, placing tinder with great care onto the growing flame. The dead turtle lay nearby as neither he nor Misha could stomach the idea of raw tortoise.

A great deal of the animal got wasted, in part to Jake not knowing how to dress tortoise and the lack of a good knife, but eventually, hunger was replaced with full, satisfied bellies.

Together they walked toward the water cliff, Misha declaring that she would climb the sharp rocks herself.

Jake could not bear to let her cut her tender fingers and insisted he carry her once more, to which she stated she was not thirsty, which was untrue for the tortoise had made them both very thirsty.

"You need to drink, and the rocks are sharp." She didn't move. "We'll find a better place to drink tomorrow." He turned his back, hunching over. "And we need to get back to the fire soon."

Slowly, she wrapped her arms around his neck, her thick hair falling over his shoulders and chest. She had to just hang for she could not wrap her legs around his waist, hindering his climb, nor would she even dare consider such an idea even if it were possible. Within minutes they were on the ledge beside the tiny pool of trickling fresh water.

They both drank extensively, pausing to watch the moon rise as the fire flickered below. Jake had dragged the tortoise back to where they had first come ashore, wanting to be near the only water they'd found.

"You kept my life," Misha said quietly, gazing at his bleeding fingers. "The night ship sink."

Jake thought back to that strange night, still wondering why and how. Misha had said nothing when he had asked, offering no information about her father or how she ended up alone in the dark waters.

"Why were you alone?" he tried again. "Alone without a life jacket?"

She said nothing.

"But you were on the upper decks, near the lifeboats. Your bodyguards… where were they?"

For a long time, she did not answer, so Jake waited, knowing he'd already asked too much.

Then she softly said, "I had to escape them."

"Escape? Who?"

"The men who sink the ship." Her words trailed off as she lowered her head in shame. "They were after me."

Jake sat speechless. "Someone… sunk… the ship?"

Misha nodded. "You saw my guards. They knew something was a fish."

"A fish?"

"Yes, something… smelly like fish."

"Smelled fishy," Jake said, smiling briefly. "Who's after you?"

She sat silent. Jake waited, but nothing more came. Eventually, they climbed back down, careful as he neared the bottom.

Jake brought the grass bedding and placed it near the fire, rolling a large bundle of grass for a pillow. He nodded for Misha to try it out. She stretched out and smiled.

The fire brought such new hope as the stars slowly joined the moon that glistened off the rolling waves, ever turning sand up and down the beach. A steady breeze kept the fire snapping, its soft caress moving over their weary bodies. The stress of the shipwreck, the days at sea crammed into a barrel, the swim through jellyfish, and the rigors of the day, followed by making a fire and butchering a tortoise, had all taken their toll.

With the fire crackling between them, each staring into the clear night of glowing stars, they lay in silence, enjoying the sounds of surf and rustling breeze.

Jake rubbed his hands, sore from climbing the cliff, and blistered from starting the fire. He sighed, closing his eyes to feel her tender skin against his back, her arms around his neck. He saw her again, cradled in his arms, hastening her to the water, his strength evaporating with the burning sun.

She's a princess, way out of your league, mountain boy. "What if we never leave?" he internally argued. "If we're never rescued?"

He shook his head. *Find a way… get her back home… safe.*

"But cherish every moment…"

Misha lay on her side, watching the bare-chested young man, his tawny muscles reflecting the fire's light. She liked his blue eyes and blond hair, so different from her everyday world. She liked his freedom, freedom to speak what he thought, to act on what he felt was right.

She admired his confidence. In all their struggles, he had pushed through. When all seemed lost, he kept moving forward, finding a solution, finding water and food, and now fire.

She had watched him carve the wood to receive the stick that he pushed back and forth for hours till the heat made the tiny ember. She had yearned to help, happy to gather fronds and bits of wood as he instructed. He was a good man. She sighed, a glimmer of hope and peace touching her anxious heart.

She nodded ever so slightly. *Yes… he makes me… feel safe.* A weak, weary smile touched her lips as she watched him, already asleep. *I should not feel this,* she warned herself. *Better to not feel this.*

She grimaced, a spike of fear rushing through her. What of the men who had come to take her? *Are they still looking? Of course, they are.*

A NEW HOME
9

WHEN MISHA OPENED HER EYES, Jake was gone, but the fire burned bright and full, the sun still a faint glow below the horizon of endless blue. She lay listening to the sounds, wondering what this new day would bring.

"Found a little breakfast," Jake called, coming up the beach with a large banana leaf full of round white balls. "Look, turtle eggs."

He placed them near the fire, digging a hole in the sand below the coals. "Followed the tracks. Just laid this morning. What'd ya think? You eat eggs?"

Misha rubbed her eyes and then stretched wide, pushing her chest out toward the rising sun. Jake stared. She abruptly stopped her stretch and covered herself.

"I'll go look for more food," he muttered, his face flushed. He couldn't go far, as the eggs would cook in minutes, so he wandered in random circles, cursing himself.

The only thing I have to look at… the absolute… most beautiful woman I have ever been with… and I can't look. Well… at least not that way. Seriously… I mean… Why does she have to be so…

"Argh, this has got to be a dream." He shook his head and sighed.

Spinning around he went to check on the eggs, careful not to look anywhere in her direction.

As they ate, he yearned to apologize, to explain how she was really beautiful and he was a guy and all and…

They ate in silence, staring out toward the sea. Knowing she wouldn't let him carry her up the drinking cliff again, he suggested searching for water before seeking more food. Misha nodded.

After gathering more wood and forming walls around the fire to slow the burn, they set off in search of water. When Jake found a trail that led toward the hills, he bent down.

"Small animal tracks… may lead to water."

Following the trail for half an hour, they came to an opening high up the side of the mountain that overlooked their now tiny beach far below. It gave a grand view of the landscape that spread far in each direction.

"A fat island," Misha said. "Very big."

Jake chuckled, quickly checking himself to then look solemn. "Yes, a big island."

He turned to move further up, but narrowed his eyes, straining to see through a grove of small trees. He walked ahead a bit, then stopped.

"Misha, come look!"

Formed into the face of a cliff wall, sat a cave the size of a small room, its opening facing toward the rising sun. A sand floor filled the smooth, level bottom—a perfect place with a splendid view.

"Come on!" Jake called, running to the cave.

Smiling wide, he spun about as Misha stepped slowly inside, her eyes taking it all in.

"What do you think?" he asked, bubbling with excitement. "We can see for miles, watch for ships, be safe from rain and other critters. Keep the fire going too."

Misha stood silent, her soul perplexed. Although it was ideal, could she sleep here in this cave, alone with this young man? For some reason, it felt different than the open beach. It was… enclosed… like a room… *like a bedroom!*

"I'll bring the fire up," Jake said. "A bit of a hike, but…" He stopped, seeing her consternation. "You okay?"

Misha suddenly staggered, head feebly wagging. Her entire world seemed to be collapsing. *Okay…?* Tears moistened her eyes. *No, I am not okay! My father may be dead. Evil men search for me. I have no clothes… and you…*

Jake watched, totally confused, heart still beating with

excitement at the discovery.

She stared at him, eyes blurring with tears. She had spent days now with an infidel, speaking to him alone without her father's consent, speaking to him with bare arms and legs, dressed in the scanty clothes of a harlot.

The tears welled as she stood trembling, eyes locked on Jake still standing inside the cave. A storm raged in her heart—one part wanting to run far away, back to her home, her normal life, where all was safe… and controlled… and so dull… —the other yearning to stay, a strange yearning she could not understand, to not only be inside this cave with Yake Connor, but to lay beside him, close beside him, wrapped within his arms.

Bursting into a sob, she turned and ran, tears trailing as she stumbled back down the hill toward the beach.

Jake watched, bewildered, then cursed himself. "But what did I do?" he grumbled with arms spread.

He looked about the cave. "This is perfect! What does she not like about this?"

He glanced down at the sandy floor. "Oh…" he said slowly. "If I were her, wearing only… yeah, would I sleep in here with me?"

He sighed, taking a moment to check the far end of the cave. "Got to find her some clothes," he said, starting to head back down after Misha. "Probably feels like one of those dreams… going to school in your underwear."

He paused to look about, recalling his vow to never let her leave his sight. "But if there's water up here…"

He turned, going further up the trail. "She's not just

a girl on the beach," he preached to himself. "She's a sheik's daughter, a princess… a *Muslim* princess."

He trudged on. "Don't stare. Don't even glance, no matter what she's doing… or how she's stretching… or standing… walking, or… argh!" He wagged his head, realizing how much he enjoyed just watching her, being with her, talking with her.

He huffed a groan. "Totally not fair." He paused to glance back, still shaking his head. "You're marooned with a real princess, Jake Connor… cowboy up!"

Feeling he'd gone too far, leaving her alone too long, he turned back only to suddenly stop. He slowly turned about, listening.

"Water! I hear water!"

Jogging over a slight hill he stopped in awe to face the most inviting sight known to man. The path of sand led right to a pool of tranquil azure water nestled beneath a ring of lush cliffs. A small steady fall of fresh mountain water poured into the pool looking like something straight from a travel brochure.

"Got to be dreaming." He walked to the edge, hesitating to put his dirty toe into the rich blue and green, its edges lined with ferns and flower-bearing shrubs. "This can't be real." With a heavy sigh of joy and relief, he knelt and drank.

After another long drink and a pause to take it all in, he jumped to his feet and ran down the hill like a child at the park, yelling for Misha to come and see.

Although reluctant and with tight-lipped silence, she followed him back. When she topped the hill, shock and wonder held her gaze, her eyes taking in the lush beauty. A fish jumped, startling her. Jake clapped his hands with delight.

"We can fish," he said, climbing a ridge overlooking the pool, squinting to see down to the depths. "What do ya think?" He suddenly realized it was the same question as at the cave. "I mean, if you want to sleep down on the beach, that's cool, we can do that. We just have to walk up here for water and there might be animals coming here…" He let it trail off, waiting for some response, trying to suppress his excitement.

She watched him come down, following his every move, her large brown eyes, intelligent, yet young. Jake approached, keeping his distance.

"I just want what's best for you," he said, his voice soft and meek. "I think the cave would be safer. I think I can find more food up here, and we have the water to drink and bath and…" He sighed. "Whatever you decide, I'll work with it." He turned to look for something to fashion into a spear for fishing.

"Yake," she said softly, "if you think cave is best, then let us… move to cave." Her insides felt tumultuous as she spoke the words, especially the word, 'us.'

Jake bowed his head as if receiving a command from his queen, then hurried them down the mountain.

TORTOISE SOUP
10

THE NEXT THREE DAYS passed quickly, as now with fire, water, and shelter, their only quest was food and keeping watch for any ship, plane, or smoke—anything that may bring rescue.

Jake had learned to stand still in the pool, holding his long, split-shaft spear that closed like jaws over the fish. More effective than a single pointed spear, a tiny stick held the toothed jaws apart, which broke when striking a fish, releasing the jaws upon the sides like barbed clamps.

The tortoise shell became a sink, bucket, and bowl.

Large clamshells became plates and bowls. He had found something like sweet potatoes and chive-like herbs. That evening, he made tortoise soup as a light rain fell outside the cave. Sitting with Misha near the fire, sipping the hot broth as the sun poked through, spreading a rainbow out across the sea, he felt like a king, the king of Sunset Isle, named by the elegant, beautiful Princess of Lahar, the most gorgeous woman to walk planet Earth. This was indeed paradise.

Misha smiled at the rainbow. For three nights she had slept inside the cave with the young man, Yake. When speaking to herself, she no longer referred to him as the infidel. He was a protector, a provider. *My protector,* she thought with both angst and subtle joy. Not once had he looked improperly at her, nor had he conducted himself in any way other than with chivalry and goodwill.

Everything womanly in her wanted to trust this man with her life. She smiled as she watched the rainbow paint the sky and sea. *Have I not already done that?* she pondered. *And has he not proved himself rather capable?*

Still, she must keep herself on guard. *I am of royal blood,* she argued, lifting her chin, squaring her shoulders. *He is nothing more than…* She let go a soft sigh. *He is… noble… more noble than any man in my father's service.* Thinking of the man her father had chosen for her, she found herself defending Jake. *More virtuous than any of those self-seeking mules.*

Her face darkened, recalling the horrible shipwreck. She thought of her uncle's son, the fiend who murdered hundreds, who came to steal her, to make her his wife by force, sinking a whole ship of innocent souls, souls now dead… because of her.

"You okay?" Jake asked, looking on with concern.

Misha startled. "Yes. Thank you for soup. It taste very good." She smiled. "You surprise me, Yake Connor."

"Jake, not Yake."

"Yyyyake!"

"Put your tongue behind your teeth."

"Lake."

"No, it has to close the air off and…" He chuckled. "Call me what you like."

She cocked her head in thought. "Khabe delam."

"What does that mean?"

A mischievous smile briefly touched her lips, eyes twinkling.

It all seemed too good—the cave, the pool, actually finding food, even though they were often hungry, not starving, just always on the quest. They talked of rescue, what form it might appear, and what to look for.

The idea to build a craft to venture back out to sea was met with a vigorous denial from Misha, who, not fully able to swim, found no comfort in the idea of wandering aimless at the mercy of the waves.

A routine settled in, with chores and duties, checking places for food and signs of animal life. Misha found some dark berries which they first tested in small portions, pleased the welcome fruit brought no ill effects. Jake had seen goats high up in the hills, walking with ease on what looked like sheer cliffs far too high for his tastes.

Little by little they adapted, always on their food quest, and always watching the sea.

One evening, Misha was particularly melancholy, looking with sad eyes out over the sea. She barely touched her freshly grilled fish.

"Do you think me… attractive?" she asked, out of the blue.

"You're joking!" Jake laughed in reply.

Instantly, her face fell. Dropping the fish, she jumped up and ran from the cave, nearly stumbling down the path to the waves.

For a moment he sat stupefied. Then cursing himself, he ran out, calling after her. The sun had dropped behind the mountains, drawing the blanket of night up over Sunset Isle, up over Misha, Princess of Lahar, and Jake, *the world's biggest idiot!*

For three hours he searched, calling till his voice grew hoarse, searching every place he felt she might go. Angst grew within as he cursed himself.

"Tact. Ever heard of tact? Ever heard of thinking before you open your trap?" He cursed. "Can't believe I didn't see that coming."

He called for her again, his voice pleading, a weak pathetic call, begging her to show herself, to not spend the night alone. He tried to tell her how he vowed that day, to never let her out of his sight, to protect her with his life if need be. The words fell onto empty darkness.

Around midnight, he shuffled back to the cave, only to stand dumbfounded, as Misha lay sound asleep beside the fire.

Crawling onto his mat, he whispered his apology. "I'm so sorry, Misha." He paused, listening to her long, steady breaths. "You are the most beautiful woman I have ever known or been near," he whispered. "Do I think you're attractive? You are tormentingly attractive. You have no idea how much…" He sighed. "…how glad I am that you're safe."

THE POOL
11

WHEN JAKE AWOKE, Misha was gone. He went to the pool and washed his face, looking about for where she might be. Taking the ridge above the pool, he dropped over to the gorge where he'd seen some rodents that moved slow enough to spear.

He had made a long spear with a burned tip, hoping to pierce one, otherwise, he would work on setting traps or making a bow. After twenty minutes of nothing, he climbed out of the gorge and stood above the pool.

In the azure waters below, bathed Misha, her fraying silk top and shorts drying in the morning sun. Her back was to him, using his *Big Sky* t-shirt as a wash towel. In the past, she had made him walk the beach when wanting to bathe. She must have thought he was there now.

A battle waged in Jake as he watched her lovely form, his heart thumping. But even before he could chide or excuse his actions, a faint shadow, long and twisty, wavered near the falls.

Flock of birds, Jake thought, watching her rinse her hair, flinging it back with a spray toward the falls.

The shadow remained. He watched her bathe, her smooth skin reflecting on the pool's tranquil water. The shadow moved, gliding out from the cliff wall, a long snake-like darkness that slithered in the depths.

Jake stepped forward to watch the shadow, heart now slamming his chest. Misha turned, saw him, and screamed. Covering herself, she shouted at him in irate Farsi. He heard none of it, his eyes on the long, thick shadow moving straight toward Misha.

Leaping hard, he sprang from the ridge, spear in both hands. The shadow shot across the pool, its head nearing the surface. In a flailing splash, he hit, his leg striking thick slimy flesh. When he broke the surface, Misha was still spewing bitter words.

He flung the water from his face just as she disappeared, her cry cut short as she went under, jerked beneath the waters of paradise.

Jake dove to see Misha thrashing as the coils of a giant gray snake already encircled her thin waist. Huge and thick, the creature began dragging her to the depths.

For one horrid moment, their eyes met. The terror in

the girl's eyes numbed his soul. Already descending into the depths, the long snake squeezed life from her lungs.

Jake thrust his spear, hitting nothing. Frantic, he kicked hard, swimming after the beast and Misha. He grabbed at the slimy skin, clutching nothing. The last of its tail slid just below him, the serpent gliding fast toward the dark waters beneath the falls.

Using both hands, Jake thrust, a rage-fired stab that plunged the spear deep into the gliding tail. He pushed and twisted the wooden shaft, driving it through, into the sandy bottom.

Instantly the water clouded as blood and sand swirled, beast and man wrestling beneath the waves that now rocked the pool of paradise. The snake had released its prey, spreading its jaws to strike the man pinning its tail. In a piercing bite, the jaws locked onto Jake's arm, jerking him like a dog with a doll, pulling him down to the depths.

To keep from being dragged down, he held his spear tight, glimpsing the dark shadow of Misha floating lifeless in the murky pool. Iron jaws crushed his left arm, jerking, pulling, tearing at the socket. Clinging to his spear, his lungs now burned, left arm screaming.

When he yanked the spear free, the loosed tail swept his feet from under him. Dragging him by the arm, it whipped him about, aiming for the depths.

Jake thrust his spear, his breath all but gone. In a desperate jab, he'd run the point under the jaw, piercing the creature's throat. Blood now swirled as the spear tore from his grasp.

He pushed for the surface, engulfed in a swirl of murk and blood. Gulping air, he then dove.

Finding Misha, he pulled her limp body up and out, dragging her onto the beach, dragging her back over the sandy path to the top of the hill, far from the pool and its slimy monster of death.

There he collapsed, his arm dripping red, whole body trembling.

What followed remains a blur. Pushing, pounding, breathing, crying, screaming, turning her over his knee, doing any and all he could contrive to bring her life back. When all seemed lost, he cast himself over her lifeless form, begging God for her return.

Spinning about, he suddenly froze. For slithering from the pool, the wretched serpent emerged. For one brief moment, their eyes met, each dripping fresh blood.

Jake could not breathe, could not move. Cold eyes locked on his. Then the creature turned and disappeared beneath the brush.

Cursing in rage, Jake screamed after the monstrous fiend that stole his love, his only joy, his sole reason for living.

"Curse you, demon of hell! I shall hunt you till the day I die!"

With bitter tears, he fell upon the lifeless Misha. Sobbing like a small boy, he pleaded with God, of whom he did not believe, or did he? He begged, promising anything and everything, pledging loyalty to God, and to this princess, if he could have but one more day with her, just one more day.

"Why take *her*?!" he screamed to the sky. "Take me!"

Fearing the giant snake would return, he hoisted her over his shoulder and ran back to the cave. Clutching her legs to his chest, he wept as he ran. Her limp body, bent and bouncing over his shoulder, hung like a broken doll—long arms dangling, hair tips sweeping the sandy path behind.

By the time he reached the cave, his legs burned with fire. He stumbled, collapsing hard onto Misha, nearly crushing her chest.

To his surprise, she coughed, then gasped, her whole frame convulsing, but only for a moment. Again her body went completely limp, face so pale and lifeless.

Jake stared, watching, hoping, but she didn't move. Bitterness filled his being. The mournful wail that rose from his soul seemed to make the very air quiver. Bitter tears poured from his eyes.

"Why?" he cried. "Why do you keep doing this to me?" He opened his mouth to utter his final curse at God when suddenly Misha's arms twitched. A moment later, they jerked, then flailed, her legs and feet then kicking wildly. After a huge choking gasp, she jerked upright, coughed, inhaled, then screamed.

Jake sat back, stunned, afraid to believe the gift of life before him. Misha continued to thrash, still in battle with the serpent. When she saw him staring, his eyes huge, she glanced about the cave totally bewildered. Then, breaking into a hard sob, she flung her arms around him.

They cried together, trembling as they tried to process the trauma.

"I'll get your clothes," Jake said, still winded. But she held him all the tighter, pressing her face into his neck.

"Do not leave me, Yacov," she said, still sobbing, "Please…"

Jake held her close, staring at the cave wall, his hands quivering. "I'm so sorry," he said softly. "Never again… will always… keep you safe."

She sniffled, gently nestling her cheek into his neck. Then, feeling the fresh blood on his arm, she gasped, "You bleed!"

BODY

12

FOR THREE DAYS Jake searched, roaming the hills, following the trail of blood and slime, determined to kill the foul beast. Misha would not set foot near the pool, drinking from the tortoise shell filled daily by Jake. They spoke little of that day, with Jake acting as if the brief moment of intimacy had never happened.

On the fourth day, Jake came back with a young goat over his shoulders, its front leg broken and swollen. To his surprise, Misha made a splint of sticks and sinewy bark. Jake watched with profound interest as she then fed the young doeling bits of grass and herbs, making a mash from the sweet potatoes, which she spoon-fed using a shell.

Jake tried to make a pen of woven sticks but Pearls, as named by Misha for her small white dots, would find escape and hobble to the cave, bleating loudly for more of Misha's mash.

"What will you do with her?" Misha asked one day.

Jake shrugged. "Fatten her up and eat her, I suppose." He suppressed a smirk as Misha's eyes grew wide with alarm. "Or we can let her go," he said smiling, to which she gave a hard swat.

Treating sunburn had been an ongoing challenge, besides the endless quest for food, but now the bright red infection spreading over Jake's arm became the main concern.

Misha insisted he rest, ending his search for the serpentine beast, allowing his body to heal. Jake found a vein of rock salt, which he added to water boiled in a tortoise shell, soaking his arm several times a day. Although it took time from hunting and gathering, it brought the redness down.

When an intense fever finally put Jake on his back, Misha went to her knees, praying in desperation, pleading with Allah to spare the ignorant young man with such a noble heart.

For a whole night and day, he faded in and out, smelly puss oozing from the horrid wound. Using Jake's t-shirt, she knelt beside him, wiping his face and forehead with cool water, to which he moaned senseless mutterings.

She did all she could—dabbing the wound with hot,

saline water, spoon-feeding him broth, pouring water down his throat, even braving a visit to the pool, all while keeping a hungry little doeling fed and out of trouble.

One evening, as rain pattered the palms outside the cave, she lay listening to the feverish moans, her tears dripping to the mat.

She realized he might very well die. Dark, foreboding scenes played through her mind, fears of seeking food while pursued by the slithering beast, taken alive once more into its iron grasp.

The horrid image of Jake's lifeless body lying here in the cave, gray with death, caused her to shudder, clammy chills leaving her skin and her soul deathly cold.

As darkness settled over the lonesome Isle of Sunset, she pulled her legs up tight, and rocking back and forth she cried long into the dreadful night.

When she awoke, Jake was gone. In panic-filled pleas, she went about, calling his name, fearing the worst, that he had wandered off in a feverish daze, lost or drown, or even taken by the beast.

She found him sitting in the pool, splashing water over his face and head. She stopped to stare with hands on her hips.

"I thought you lost," she said, scolding him like a naughty child.

He smiled weakly at the dark-haired maiden, her eyes weary and sunken.

"Thanks," he said, coming out to sit on the smooth sand. He gazed at the gentle waterfall surrounded by a beautiful array of blooming orchids. She came and sat beside him, studying his red, swollen arm.

"You feel better?"

He nodded. "Fever's gone."

"Are you hungry?"

"Starving."

"That is most good!" she said, excited. Then she slumped, her lip in a pout. "But... we have no food."

"I saw ripe bananas up that way. But my arm... Can you climb?"

"Me?"

Jake chuckled. "I'll find something... somewhere."

Walking the beach together, watching the sun cut through the morning mist, they found tortoise tracks that led to eggs. Jake caught a small crab in a splash pool and Misha found two ripe coconuts. They were about to turn back to the cave and make their strange breakfast when Misha cried out with alarm.

"Yake! Look!"

Rolling in the surf near the rocks, a body sloshed about, dark tattered clothes clinging to its mangled limbs. With anything but eagerness, Jake pulled the body from the surf.

Disfigured and horrid, the mangled form of a man, once dressed in a suit of black, lay sprawled on the sand. Misha covered her mouth and turned away. Jake suppressed an urge to heave as he studied the mutilated flesh. He scanned the body.

A belt of leather, and shoestrings… cloth for sunburn, pants cut into shorts for Misha… He shook himself, a bit unnerved by his thoughts.

A large watch still clung to the gnawed wrist. Gingerly, Jake slid the watch from the body, holding it up toward the sun.

"Still ticking," he said with a wry chuckle, handing it for Misha to see. She shook her head in disgust, then suddenly gasped.

"What is it?" Jake asked.

Her eyes grew wide with alarm as she searched the face of the mangled body.

"That's Murik's watch," she said in a low voice, her feet shuffling backward.

"Who's Murik?"

For a long time she stood, hands over her mouth. "He is, was, head of security, my father's bodyguard… *my* bodyguard."

Although badly gnawed, the body could not have been drifting since the wreck. That was over eleven days ago. Then Jake saw what could only be a bullet hole, a small hole in the right temple, the other temple looking, well, rather messy.

"He was murdered," Jake said quietly. "Murdered recently." He looked up at Misha.

She slowly shook her head, backing further from the horrid body. Seeing her physically tremble, he took her away, back toward the cave.

After a few steps, she stopped him. "You cannot leave him as this. You must…"

"I'll take care of him. Let's get you back to the cave."

His mind raced with questions. They had talked little of that night and her predicament. Jake had learned she was pledged to marry a certain prince of Karaj, but her uncle's son, Torik, wanted her like a madman wants the world.

Jake wondered if the uncle's men had taken out the radio before sinking the ship, making sure no one survived, that no one could know they had taken Misha. She would have just disappeared into his harem.

But people survived. And this guy must have talked.

After their breakfast of tortoise eggs, scraps of crab, and laboriously gotten coconut milk, Jake went to bury the body. He was quite surprised when Misha followed.

"Are you sure?"

"He was a good man."

Jake asked her not to look as he tried to strip the body, able to take only the leather belt and shoelaces. Although the clothes were greatly needed and still very useable, he could not bring himself to take them off, repressing the urge to vomit every other minute.

He rolled the body of Murik into a shallow trench. Still weak from the bout with infection, he could do little more than spread a coat of sand on top.

As he worked the sand around the grave, he caught a glint of light from where the corpse had lain. To his great delight, he held a large folding knife up for Misha to see, then belted out a victorious cry that frightened the birds watching the odd funeral.

"A knife, Misha, a knife!" He did a little jig beside the

grave. "Was on his belt. I almost missed it." But seeing her solemn face, he suppressed his joy and continued the work of burying Murik, head of security for the sheik of Lahar.

"I'll come back later," he huffed, "when I feel better." Strapping on the belt, he snugged up his tattered cargo shorts, reveling in the weight of the knife hanging in all its power and glory.

Misha spoke some words in Farsi, tears dropping freely from her lovely eyes. She had picked an orchid on their way down, which she now placed with tender care on the shallow grave.

They stood in silence beneath the palms, listening to the ever-present surf as a few gulls circled and moved on.

"You think him murdered," she asked as they walked back.

"Yes. And only a few days ago."

She walked in silence back to the cave where she sat on her mat, knees to her chest, solemn eyes staring out over the sea. It was a beautiful view, a perfect place to put a cave, if one chose to live in a cave on a tropical island in the middle of the sea.

Jake fondled the knife, opening and closing its five-inch blade. Misha said something to herself, softly sniffling. Jake moved beside her, longing to comfort her, to wrap an arm around her. But they sat in silence, watching the sea.

"He looks for me," she finally said. "Torik seeks for me."

"May think you're dead," Jake said hopefully, "went down with the ship."

She shook her head. "He saw me jump."

Jake sat upright, a whole new view of Misha now emerging. She couldn't really swim, barely enough to float. Yet she had jumped? A princess of luxury, surrounded by bodyguards, had chosen to jump, to risk her life rather than endure an alternate fate.

Though bursting with questions, Jake waited, consigned to receive only what she willingly gave.

Misha knew he had questions, was eager for answers. Yet he never prodded. She appreciated that. Saw it as respect. In her world of wealth and high society, she was respected but only by obligation. She never felt truly respected as a person, except by her mother.

She looked over at Jake's dirty bare feet, then at her own—once painted toenails now chipped and lined with dirt. They certainly weren't in high society here. Yet this young man from Montana shows more true respect than anyone, besides her mother.

After a time of silence, she told how they had received word of Torik's plot to kidnap her, so the wedding got moved forward and the location changed, thus the trip to Vanuatu. However, they had underestimated the madness of Torik, never thinking he would sink the ship with all its passengers.

"So… you're engaged?" Jake asked, his voice betraying him.

She slowly nodded. "But I not love him. It was arranged by Father." She turned to look at Jake, dark shadows encircling his sunken eyes. His arm had turned a purplish-red with puss still oozing. "You must to rest," she said, seeing the strain this added. She rose, motioning him to lie down. "I will heat water... for your arm."

Jake watched her place a large shell on a stand they had made over the fire, which worked rather well.

Like poetry in motion, he thought, referencing an old hit from the sixty's. She moved with such grace that even in the tattered t-shirt she was simply entrancing.

Exhausted, wishing to sleep for a hundred years, he watched her move about, yearning like never before to tell her what he really felt. *But how can I? She's a princess... a Muslim princess, pledged to wed a man she doesn't love... hunted by a madman who's killed to make her his own.*

"And will keep killing," he said to himself, a host of new fears creeping in.

Misha stirred the fire, her long wavy hair pulled to one side.

"I can do that," Jake said, straining to sit up.

"No, you cannot," she said firmly. "Lay down."

Jake lay back with a sigh. *How will this end?* he wondered, rather fearfully, thinking mostly of Misha.

How could Jake, the infidel, the guy already breaking every cultural law just being near her, say anything endearing to one such as Misha of Lahar?

"You're beautiful," he murmured. She pretended not to hear, again telling him to lay back. He closed his eyes, her touch gentle on his wounded arm.

PARADISE OF DESPAIR
13

HE SLEPT THE REST of that day, waking when the sun had set. They had nothing for food so they lay waiting for the light of day, listening to their bellies groan, talking little as Misha mourned the death of Murik. She had known him for as long as she could remember. He was always kind—stern and unyielding, but kind.

The next day, they hiked up to where Jake had seen a grove of banana trees that held several bunches of small ripe bananas.

"Found this the other day," he said, "before I fell sick."

He tied the belt between his ankles and climbed the tree in a hopping fashion, the belt catching the bark, holding as he hopped up a foot at a time. With great joy, he sliced a bunch free and dropped them to Misha. She surprised him, as he did not think she would actually catch them.

While in the tree he saw something that again caused him to exclaim with great joy.

"Mangos!" he called down, pointing to a tree higher up toward the mountain.

They hiked some time before they found a trail that led toward the large mango tree.

Something had eaten the lower fruit and cleaned up what had fallen. So, using mostly one arm, Jake climbed the trunk. When he came back down with a bunch of mangoes hanging from his belt, his smile shone from ear to ear. Beaming like a young boy, he took the knife and peeled the yellow skin, handing Misha a large slice of fresh ripe mango. He watched her eat, laughing as the juice dripped from her lips.

She smiled, even giggling as the taste of the sweet, juicy fruit filled her aching stomach.

They ate too much and suffered for it, with pains that came and went over the next hour. But the joy it brought far outweighed any adverse effects.

Jake walked with pride. He had a knife. He could and would provide for and protect his Persian princess, the beautiful Misha of Lahar.

They were far above the cave and pool, higher than they ever had climbed. Misha lay back, stretching her arms out over her head, something Jake wished she would not do. Misha looked at him and smiled. It seemed like an invitation. He scooted close, struggling to keep his hands at his side.

"Those were delicious," he said, his heart suddenly pumping a bit too fast. *You look delicious,* he thought, ordering himself not to say or do something stupid.

But it was a beautiful day, their bellies finally satisfied, both relaxing close together, enjoying a breeze that rose from the surf. Puffy clouds hung above as the ocean spread out as far as they could see, its lush blue-green, framing their little paradise with vibrant beauty. If ever there was a time to tell her how he felt…

She sighed, all stretched out on the grassy knoll, her slender fingers fiddling with her hair. "A paradise," she said, her face glowing as she smiled at Jake.

She looked dreamily beautiful. Jake watched with blood warming, his heart beating faster with each breath. He wet his lips, eyes fixed on hers—so full, so inviting. *No, you fool! She's out of your league.* He tried to hold back the heat flushing his face, his chest, his whole body. But his breathing betrayed him.

Misha sat up quickly, an arm over her chest, the other gathering her long legs upward. A stern expression tightened her face, but suddenly dropped as her eyes went wide.

"Look!" she cried.

Pointing to the north, she stood with arm fully outstretched. Jake jumped to his feet. Far to the north, in the distant haze, sat the tiny form of a ship. For a full minute, they just stood watching it move ever so slowly toward the east.

Jake spun about in a mad frenzy. "Wood... signal fire," he said, speaking too fast. "But the fire's in the cave." He glanced up, squinting at the distant ship. "It's too far... would never see it." Then back to spinning about, he muttered, "Smoke, lots of smoke."

But all was lush green, not even a single dried frond. He stopped to stare once more at the tiny ship. "Would they even come?" he said, thinking aloud. "Change coarse... for some smoke?"

Even if he ran, it would take over a half hour to reach the cave. He slumped.

Standing together in silence, they watched it pass. As it disappeared into the horizon, a thick, heavy loneliness settled over them. Their gorgeous day had slipped into shadow, a shadow that darkened into deep despair.

They weren't in paradise. They were stranded, trapped like animals, where every day could be their last, where life hung in the quest for food, in avoiding danger, in staying sane.

Jake weakly wagged his head. They could spend the rest of their lives watching ships pass by, watching in silent despair as hope dwindled with each endless day, always struggling to eat, struggling to stay alive.

Together they trudged down the hill back to the cave, walking in solemn silence. A new enemy, unseen, had arrived on their island, that silent killer—despair.

NEW HOPE
14

FOR TWO DAYS they went about their usual quest, Jake having found but a few crabs and a fish to go with some greens and a few bananas. He had not hiked back to the mango tree, as bitterness had taken his soul, blaming the mangos for all that happened or rather didn't happen.

A voice taunted, denouncing him for being such a wimp. *Be a man! Tell her! Heck, show her! She wouldn't be alive if you hadn't saved her.*

He shook his head, but some dark anger kept trying

to rise. *You've risked your life, man. You've earned her. It's only right you should—*

"Shut up!" He thrust his spear into a rotting stump. "I don't deserve squat. Should never have pulled her into that stupid barrel."

That night something took their goat, leaving nothing but splotches of blood. For two days, Jake walked about with a scowl, saying little to Misha.

Though only nineteen, she knew enough to understand the troubled mind of a young man, and with a wisdom beyond most, she sought him out.

She found him sulking by the pool, and sat down beside him, offering dried mango, which she'd sliced and dried in the sun.

"How is your arm?" she asked.

"Better."

But for the birds ever squawking and whistling, a silence held the man and woman sitting side-by-side, watching the water that poured over the rocks into the pool, a peaceful bubbling that stirred the tranquil waters, which just a week before had brought such terror.

"Never I know a man like you, Yake Connor," she said softly as if to herself. She sat quiet for a while, twirling a lock of her hair. "There is..." She sighed. "I wish much to tell you..." She paused, moist eyes studying his profile. He had trimmed his beard with the knife, leaving a scruffy stubble.

Jake looked up, a flicker of hope trying to rise, but he snuffed it out, rebuking himself bitterly.

She blinked back tears. "I wish..." she said again, her

eyes pooling. "Oh, Yacov, we must get off island." She touched the back of his hand. "Please… get me off island… so I can…" She now squeezed his hand. "…can tell you what my heart is crying."

Jake straightened, his eyes alert. "Tell me what?" he asked urgently.

She shook her head, tears trailing. "Please find a way," she said in a soft whisper, "a way for us…" She delicately wiped her eyes. "For you and me to leave Isle of Sunset. Please…"

Biting her lip, she rose, snuffling some, but with dignity.

Jake watched her in total bewilderment, suddenly realizing how thin she had become. Then he stood and faced her, gently taking her by the shoulders.

"I'll find a way," he said, his stare intense, "or I will die trying."

With new vigor, he set traps, channeled fish into a pen of sticks near the falls, climbed for mangos and bananas, hunting the beaches early for tortoise and their eggs. He went to finish the burial of Murik but found the body dragged away by something powerful enough to drag a large mangled man.

Tracks of cougar-like prints surrounded the shallow grave, which explained their missing goat. New fears rose, especially for Misha. They were no longer safe inside their cave now that this cat had tasted human flesh.

Best not tell her, he thought, *just prepare.*

Sitting by the fire, sipping tea from clamshells, a tea Jake made from drying some fragrant leaves, they watched as the setting sun highlighted the clouds in the east. He looked long at Misha, her skin so smooth, her hair shining in the fire's light. He had to wonder once again if she were real.

Her lifeless body came back to mind, his desperate plea and promise to protect. He remembered again the shock of seeing her breathe, to see her thrash about, naked and bruised, blood from his arm smeared on her chest and torso.

"You're alive," he said softly.

She nodded toward his arm. "Like you."

He remembered that day, that moment she nestled into his neck. He had pleaded for just one day, one more day with Misha. He'd gotten that wish and more. He would be content to spend the rest of his life here on this island if it meant being with her.

He longed for her to be rescued—for her sake—yet for him, it most certainly meant separation. And yet her plea for him to find a way… for 'you and me.' He liked those words.

Then a thought came.

What if she ends up with the madman? Maybe she's safer here… with me? No. She wants to go home… and I promised.

"Misha…"

"Yes, Yake Connor."

"If I get us off this island…"

"Yes?"

"Will you let me visit you? Would that ever be possible?"

Without reply, she looked away, staring off toward the sea as the horizon darkened. He watched as she bit her lip, eyes welling with tears. Her lips parted as she prepared to answer, but then craned her neck, squinting toward the sea.

"Look!" She pointed toward the east. Tiny lights shone in the blue darkness. "Another ship!"

BLOOD AND FLAME
15

FOR A LONG TIME, they sat watching the glimmering lights that had not moved.

"Seems they're anchored," Jake said, a strange foreboding pressing his heart.

With equal trepidation, Misha watched, finally settling down on her grass mat, yet keeping an eye on the distant lights. Jake observed her with growing concern.

"What do you think?" he asked, to which she only shook her head.

After a while he too lay back on his grass mat, watching the stone ceiling that flickered with the last of the fire's light, his mind and heart a muddled mess.

A sound awoke them both, a dull hum out on the water. It was early dawn, the sun not yet breaking the horizon. Within minutes they could see a small craft making its way to Sunset Isle.

For a time, Jake didn't move, his heart and head still lost in a jumbled mess of conflicting feelings and tangled thoughts.

Standing in the opening of their cave home, they watched in silence as the boat approached, bouncing over the waves, a motorized raft carrying five men… all dressed in black.

Misha trembled, her nostrils flaring with each apprehensive breath.

"Time to get you home," Jake said, walking from the cave.

"Wait!" Misha stopped him, the image of Murik filling her mind. "I think we best to wait."

She's trembling, Jake noticed with rising alarm. "Okay, I'll go down. You stay out of sight." He paused. "You okay?"

Misha nodded, touching his hand. "They could be pirates. Be careful, Yacov."

He had made a stout club from a dense wood after seeing the cougar-like prints. He now took it up. "If anyone comes, you hide behind the ridge at the pool."

She nodded as he walked the path toward the beach, club in hand. A black inflatable, it now revved through the surf, its bow soon to reach the sands of Sunset Isle.

Jake jogged, keeping low, watching the crew come ashore. Cradling big guns and dressed in black military-style gear, the five men spread out immediately, as if time were in short supply.

A rescue… pirates… or something worse?

One pointed to footprints, calling for the others. Soon they were following Jake and Misha's prints up the trail toward the cave. Murik's mangled body flashed through his mind.

Something's not right. But what can I do? Who are these guys?

Never had his heart pumped so hard, except that night the ship exploded. *Are these the same guys… Torik's men?*

They now came jogging up the trail, the leader urging them on. Jake crouched low as they hustled past, pounding blood filling his ears. "Misha…" he whispered, "please be hiding. I don't like these guys."

He followed at a distance, watching with panted breaths as they searched the cave, then moved up the trail toward the pool. They seemed to be on a mission, like they knew what they were looking for and needed to find it fast.

Jake waited, listening, praying to the God that did not exist, pleading with Misha to have followed his direction, praying she'd know what to do.

In long silence he waited, unable to follow further as the trees near the pool were small and sparse.

He tried to steady his heart, to think clearly. *They could be here to rescue her. We've just grown island crazy, paranoid from being alone so long.* He had almost convinced himself when a scream came drifting down.

He raised his club, readying himself. His mind seemed to narrow, focusing on one simple drive—protect Misha.

The men came all too fast, jogging down the trail, passing the cave, the long legs of Misha kicking wildly, her torso flopped over the largest of the black-garbed men.

Jake watched in raging dread. They were *obviously* not here to rescue. And no, they weren't pirates. They could only be the same men who put Murik in the water, who sent a ship to the depths. They had come with one mission—kidnap Misha and bring her to Torik.

Void of rational thought, Jake ran behind the last of the men, his club poised to strike. When the leading men rounded a bend, he did what only a madman compelled by something stronger than life itself would do. Rushing up behind, he swung his club, striking with savage vengeance.

Wild blood pumping, he pulled the man off the trail into the brush. Again, without thought, he stripped the man, yanking off his clothes in quick, fluid movements. The soldier lay there as though dead, eyes still open, yet he groaned with each breath.

Moving like a frenzied maniac, Jake donned the soldier's pants and shirt. Snugging the belt and slinging the gun over his shoulder, he muttered a quick prayer.

"God, if you're out there… please…"

Running barefoot, he caught up as the men were already near the boat. The lead man gave orders in a foreign tongue, clearly instructing them to tie Misha and set her in the boat. Jake slowed to a hustling jog. The lead man only glanced his way, shouting and very irate. Jake slowed, his finger on the trigger.

He knew guns, but not this one. He had looked it over as he ran, knew it would fire in bursts, a bit difficult to control, and very deadly.

Two men bound Misha as he came near, the lead man giving sharp, terse orders. One had entered the Zodiac-like craft, preparing its engine.

Jake's blond hair and blue eyes would soon betray him. He had two seconds at best.

The leader looked up, immediate confusion twisting his dark features. Jake raised his weapon, aiming at the man's chest.

"Let her go!" he shouted, hands quivering.

The two binding Misha turned about. The man in the boat paused to look up. A heartbeat of silence followed.

Then the man in the boat reached for his weapon.

A burst of gunfire riddled the inflatable, the pressurized air hissing loudly. The man toppled backward, stumbling over the engine and into the surf.

When the leader raised his gun, Jake took aim, this time for the kill.

But before either could shoot, a spray of automatic fire chopped through the sand between them. Both ducked, turning away from the spitting sand. A second burst hit the inflatable, cutting it in half. Then a flash of heat burst from the craft, tossing Misha and her captors down onto the sand.

The explosion roared upward, its cloud of black and orange racing into the morning sky. Jake stood stunned, the sudden heat intense. Black soot shot high as gas, rubber, and wood burned with immense heat, swirling upward in a rumbling wind.

The leader was on his knees, toppled by the blast. He now groped for his gun while crawling from the heat.

Misha lay pinned beneath the two men, her hands still bound in front. She struggled madly, yelling angry things in Farsi.

A chopper filled the sky overhead, its thumping blades beating like war drums. A dust cloud engulfed the chaos on the beach, the leader shouting for his men.

But Jake had moved in, striking one man with his rifle butt. Aiming his gun at the other, he dragged Misha out and away.

A glob of burning rubber had fallen near her side, its flame greedily gnawing at the ragged t-shirt. Moving his gun back and forth between the leader and the other still on the sand, he dragged Misha up the beach.

When he saw the flame at her side, he dropped his gun, smothering the fire with sand.

Gunfire broke out all around him as the chopper closed in. He reached for his gun, but then scooped up Misha instead. Carrying her in his arms, he ran to the cover of the trees.

"Are you hurt?" he huffed, falling to his knees.

The gunfire had stopped rather abruptly, but the

flames still roared from the boat and fuel tank. Over-head the chopper thundered, its blades still swirling up a sand cloud.

Jake looked Misha over, surprised to see no burns, only soot and sand covering her tender skin. He slashed the rope binding her wrists, helping her sit up.

She sat panting, her whole body trembling.

Jake looked back, searching for his gun. Three men were in the surf. One lay where Jake had struck him.

He turned to retrieve his gun, but Misha clutched his arm.

"No, Yake! No!"

He dropped down beside her, kneeling, his back to a tree, the very one they had slept beneath that first night, their crude grass mats still on the sand, the blackened firepit between them.

He quickly looked her over once more, skin dirty but not burned. "Sure you're not hurt?" he asked, undoing some cording still tight about one wrist. "We have to run."

"Torik's men," she said breathless, eyes staring at the smoldering chaos. "You shoot them?" She looked up and down the uniform, stopping at his dirty bare feet. "You kill this one?"

"No, I…"

The chopper now whirled overhead, its roar echoing off the mountains. Jake jumped up, helping Misha to her feet.

"Come on!" he shouted, helping her along.

But the helicopter dropped quickly to hover over

them, tossing fronds and dust about their heads. As Jake strained to see, three men suddenly stood blocking his path, each holding an automatic weapon. He turned about, arms around Misha, shielding her tight.

RESCUED?

16

"LET ME GO!" Misha kept shouting as the blades thundered. "My father's men. Let me go, Yacov!"

Two men took Jake down hard. They dragged him toward the chopper which had landed on the beach. The other gently escorted Misha.

On the sand, a dozen yards from the burning craft, they pinned Jake down, a rough boot to his neck. Misha screamed for them to stop as a short, heavyset man with a barrel chest stepped slowly from the chopper. Jake craned to see, half his face buried in the beach.

The man walked with a swagger, his Middle Eastern

garb swirling in the chopper's wind. Grinning, he walked straight to Misha, arms wide.

Pinned down, sucking dust, Jake lay still, watching Misha weep in her father's embrace. Fear and anger still fired his blood, but to see her such, brought relief… and a trickling of sadness.

It was over.

In a crazy flash of gunfire and flame, the ordeal of Sunset Isle was finally over. Life would go back to normal. Back to…

The sadness grew.

Then Misha spun, shouting to the man whose foot held Jake captive. She continued scolding him as she extended a hand to Jake. He rose with wary eyes, heart pounding furiously.

Misha rattled off a myriad of strange words, pointing to the sea, the trees, and up toward the cliff.

In a mix of English and Farsi, she told of Jake's daring rescue, explaining his garb and the gunfight on the beach. She smiled with pride, describing the exploits of this fine young man, Yacov Connor.

But Jake saw none of her sentiment shared by the father. The hefty man only stared at the tall young man, then at the ragged t-shirt and long bare legs. He barked an order, and a soldier came running with a blanket, carefully draping it over Misha.

With a scowl, he spoke first in Farsi, then with annoyance, he repeated himself in English.

"You infidel…" he said, standing close to Jake. "You Western worm… how dare you!"

Misha stiffened. "Father?"

"Silence!" Keeping his eyes on Jake, he spoke slowly in English. "Gouge out his eyes… then drop his head into the sea."

Misha gasped.

Without blinking, the man continued. "How dare you look upon my daughter, you… pagan worm. She is not for your eyes. She is the daughter of Fariborz, glorious Sheik of Lahar."

Misha stood gaping, her scuffed face now ashen. Jake's legs went limp, his lungs stuck.

"Father," Misha cried, "you cannot! He—"

"Silence!"

"No!" Misha said sternly. "He save my life! I will not be silent! You cannot kill him!"

Taken aback, the man stared sternly at Misha, her audacious actions unprecedented. "He has defiled you!" Hot rage flooded the man's face. "Skin him!" he screamed, his head and neck quivering. "Skin him alive!"

"No! Father, no!" Misha threw herself at his feet, pleading loudly. "No! He never dishonor me!" she called out. "Never once he touch me that way. In all Persia, not find a man like Yacov Connor. He is noble, my Father. I plead his life. Suffer me no more than I have been suffered." She pressed her face to his feet, arms wrapping his legs.

Her pleas and tears seemed to stay her father's rage. Growling, he ordered them to bring Jake aboard. With a disgusted spat, he waved a hand toward the beach and the burning mass.

Jake kept his head low, glancing only once into Misha's red eyes, her dirty cheeks streaked with tears.

Not what I imagined, he grumbled, trying to judge his odds of survival. His heart ached as if he'd just run a very hard sprint.

Often he had consoled himself regarding the inevitable separation, with images of rich rewards for having saved the beautiful princess of Lahar.

What... a... joke!

The chopper landed on a yacht the size of a small cruise ship. A joyous celebration came from all aboard as Misha stepped from the chopper, her bare legs beneath her blanket wrap causing as equal commotion as her arrival.

She introduced her mother to Jake as her father continued to scowl. The woman just stared at the blue-eyed man dressed in the black garb of Torik.

In great trepidation, Jake followed orders, bathing and shaving, dressing in fine silks and slippers. For several hours he was kept alone in a room, dreading his fate. He tried to convince himself that Misha would smooth things out, but it didn't fly.

You're dead, cowboy. You failed.

He pictured them fussing over Misha, spreading out a sumptuous meal. *You're not invited, Mr. Hero,* the cynical voice pestered. *Best pray they make it quick.*

"Final meal would be nice, though," Jake muttered.

He wondered why Misha hadn't yet come to see him.

Already forgotten me, he sulked, weary from the morning's trauma. *What an idiot, thinking you could have a princess.* He gave a bitter, single laugh. *Women… love to mess with a guy's head, make him think he's got a chance, then crush him beneath their high-heeled shoes.*

It was well past noon when a man came and led him to Misha's father. Jake searched the room for Misha, cold fear prickling his spine. The hefty man sat at a small table set with coffees and dried fruit. He stared long into Jake's eyes.

Unashamed, Jake held his gaze.

Fariborz, Sheik of Lahar took a sip of black coffee. "You are filth to me," he said with his heavy accent. "You have defiled my daughter. I grant you till sunset." He made a slicing motion over one eye, and then the other, and then a sudden slice across his neck. "Misha will think you are safe in America." He flashed a conniving smile.

How could Misha have come from this guy? Jake wondered. "But I saved your dau—"

A large hand knocked him aside the head, toppling him onto a table. Coffee spilled, fruits toppling to the floor.

"Take him out!" the sheik hollered.

Two men dragged Jake out as the words, "Sunset, infidel… sunset," trailed behind him.

STANDOFF
17

WITH HANDS AND FEET tied, Jake sat in a room filled with lush silk bedding and pillows. A large, silent guard stood at the doorway. A window gave Jake a clear view of the western sky, the last sunset he would see, the last sunset of his life.

As dreadful as all had become, the greatest pain that filled his heart was for Misha. He longed to see her just one last time, to just say goodbye. But he knew that could never be, as she would be told he'd been sent to America.

Then anger rose like a burning fire. *How can this jerk*

kill the guy who saved his daughter? She wouldn't even be here if it weren't for me. The guy's an idiot, an absolute idiot.

His nostrils flared as he watched the guard, studying the pistol at his belt. He scanned the room, thinking desperately, spurring his mind to find a plan.

He stood from the chair, wiggling.

"Gotta pee," he said, nodding to the ropes, crossing his knees, and squatting.

The guard scowled, but then opened a door to a small bathroom. Jake hobbled over, holding out his hands, but the guard slowly wagged his head, giving Jake a shove and closing the door.

The bonds were of nylon rope. Jake opened a medicine cabinet behind the mirror, hoping to find something sharp, anything.

Like what? A disposable shaver? a taunting voice mocked. *Maybe some sleeping pills?*

It was empty. He knelt, checking the cabinet beneath the sink. An old yachting magazine lay in the far back corner. Jake sighed.

But as he closed the cabinet door, a glint of light flashed from beneath the magazine's edge. Reaching back, he found, to his surprise, an old-fashioned foldout razor, its blade gleaming bright with hope.

For a moment, he knelt staring at the shiny blade, heart racing.

Cut the ropes now or later? he pondered, fighting to stay calm. A heavy fist thumped the door. Jake shoved the razor down his pants and flushed the toilet, heart drumming ribs.

Coming from the bathroom, he asked to lie on the bed where he faced a window, watching the sun move toward the west.

After a few minutes, a knock came and the guard opened the door a few inches. The large man soon argued with a female, both voices stern as they bantered back and forth. The woman wasn't happy.

Misha!

With the guard occupied at the door, he quickly cut the ropes and slunk from the bed. Razor in hand, he snuck up behind, dreading what he must do. *Kill or be killed,* he told himself. *It's him or you.*

He stood, waiting for the right moment. Then he saw a large marble vase. As the guard gave a final word and closed the door, Jake swung the vase. To his surprise, it didn't break, but the man slumped in a crumpling thud.

For a second, Jake stood stunned, then peeked out the door, but Misha had gone. He quickly tied the man, gagging him with a pillowcase. Wrapping the pistol in a towel, he cracked open the door.

At the end of the hall stood a set of double doors, so out he went, assuming it to be Misha's bedroom. But when he looked inside, there sat her father speaking with a tall handsome man surrounded by several men in dark suits.

No one saw or heard him so he gently shut the door, wondering which way to go. He had taken only several steps when the latch turned and out came the handsome man and the guards. Jake quickly slipped through the nearest door, stopping abruptly. Three beautiful young women sat about in silks, sipping drinks, talking and laughing. They stopped as he entered, staring in silence. Jake bowed, offering a charming, yet very anxious smile.

"Excuse me," he said, "wrong room." He paused, waiting as long as he could, listening for the men to leave the hall. "Y'all have a nice day." A rush of giggling whispers followed as he closed the door.

Without knowing why, he went back to the father's room, opening the door slowly. He scanned the room, gun ready, but still hidden beneath the towel.

Misha's father sat resting, his eyes closed with head back. As Jake closed the door, the man sat up with a start. He inhaled to call out, but then held it, the gun barrel aiming straight for his face. For a moment he looked genuinely afraid, wide eyes focused on the gun.

Jake went up close. "I never touched your daughter," he said, thinking it strange to say such. "I did everything I could to help her and keep her alive. You have no right to—"

"Silence, infidel!"

At this, Jake brought the gun up to the man's forehead. With his jaw clenched tight, the young man fought hard to not yield to his anger.

"If you weren't Misha's father…" he said through clenched teeth, pressing the barrel hard into the large man's forehead. He stepped up close, driving the head backward. "And if you call me infidel one more time, I swear I will split your dimwit brains. Now, are you going to let me go or must I take your life to save mine?"

Jake stepped back, awaiting a reply.

Suddenly the door opened and in came the tall man with Misha and the men in suits. They all stopped, totally stunned. Jake stepped to the side, the gun now at the father's temple. Misha gasped.

"Yake, what you do?"

At first, Jake couldn't answer. Dressed in beautiful silks and flowing gown, Misha stood adorned like a virtual goddess. Her long hair hung in some intricate braid woven with silver thread. Her plush lips glimmered as gold glinted from earrings and bracelets.

"He's... Your father's taking my head at sunset, Misha. Taking out my eyes first." The words sounded weird.

"No, Yacov," Misha said, wagging her head. "He promise take you to America."

Jake turned to Fariborz. "Tell her the truth, Muslim."

"The infidel lies," her father said, as the guards slowly went for their guns. "He plans to steal you, my daughter."

Jake fired the pistol just above the father's head, shattering a window with a thunderous boom.

"Tell her the truth!"

"Look around you, infidel. You are a fool."

"Then we both die, Muslim. Tell them to drop their guns."

The father did not budge. Several weapons clicked in preparation. Tension held the room as Jake stood, finger ready.

Suddenly Misha drew a dagger from a guard's belt beside her. In both hands, she held it beneath her breast, aimed at her heart. Tears pooled as she cried out.

"If Yake dies, I die!"

"Misha, no!" Jake called to her.

"I give five seconds," she said to her father, her lips quivering. "Let Yacov go, or lose me, your only daughter."

"Misha... stop." Jake stared, his mind racing.

"Five... four..."

"Misha!" Jake looked to the father. The hefty man sat silent, a smug look on his plump face.

"Three... two..."

The tall handsome man, the one to whom Misha was pledged, also stood silent, just watching. A woman stepped in—Misha's mother. Seeing the standoff, she screamed.

"Father?" Misha pleaded, her voice trembling. He made no response. Misha extended her arms, preparing to thrust the dagger. Jake yelled for her to stop.

She held the dagger poised, her eyes on its gleaming point.

"Misha, please. Drop the knife. I surrender." Jake dropped to his knees, setting the gun on the floor.

Three men rushed him, guns aimed.

The father stood, rage filling his face. He kicked Jake hard in the chest. "You vile worm! How dare you?"

"Father!" Misha struggled against a man holding her arms. "How dare *you*?"

He stepped toward Misha, his arm raised.

"Stop this!" Misha's mother stepped before her husband. In rapid Farsi she jabbered, pointing at Jake, pointing at Misha, pointing at her husband, and finally pointing at the handsome man pledged to marry Misha.

Somehow, Jake knew what she was saying, that she was his defense lawyer, having heard everything from Misha, was now arguing his case.

The husband said nothing as the woman, quite beautiful and clearly intelligent, from whom Misha got her grace and elegance, spoke with irate words. She was clearly denouncing her husband regarding his treatment of the infidel who saved their daughter. She pointed one more time to the handsome man, and then her finger came to rest on Jake. She finished in English.

"Were he, not an infidel, I would deem him more worthy…" She stopped herself, lips tight, trembling with fury. The father waited till his wife had finished, nodding that he had listened.

"I am Fariborz, Sheik of Lahar. For you and Misha's sake, I will not take his eyes, nor his head, but…" He looked upon Jake with rage still building. "He has held a gun to my head, defiled my daughter and my vessel, and will, by all the powers of Allah, pay for his abominations! How dare you speak of his noble ways?"

He raised a hand to strike Jake but glancing to his wife, withdrew. "Tie an anchor to his feet. Send him to hell. As I have spoken, so it will be."

REVELATION

18

WITH MISHA DRAGGED AWAY, weeping bitterly, and the mother speaking very angry words, Jake was taken topside where his feet were bound to an iron anchor weighing at least a hundred pounds.

"Did you defile my daughter?" the father asked, speaking close to Jake's face, eyes narrowed. "Confess and I will let you live."

It didn't make any sense to Jake, but still, he did what he knew to do—speak the truth. "I never touched your daughter. I protected her."

"You lie. All infidels lie." He gave a nod to the men.

"How does a man like you have a daughter like Misha?" Jake asked in defiant boldness. "She's not yours, is she?"

Taken aback, Fariborz glared at Jake. Then rage filled his face. "You are a dog with a wayward tongue."

Jake chuckled wryly. "At least I'm not an impotent sheik."

The man's soft hand slapped Jake hard, knocking him to the deck. Blood dribbled from his lips as the men yanked him up.

"Throw him over. Silence the infidel." He said the last word slowly, spitting into Jake's face.

Two men held Jake as another slid the heavy anchor toward the edge of the deck, an open deck for diving and swimming. A rope of maybe ten feet bound his ankles, leaving his hands free. He looked about for Misha, hoping to see her just one last time. A burly man set a foot against the anchor, his eye on the sheik. A nod, a shove, and the anchor plunged into the boat's wake.

Jake jumped the instant it fell, hitting the water at almost the same moment. As bubbles swirled past, he dug for the razor in his pants. The slack tightened quickly and with a painful jerk, his body sped downward.

He struggled to reach the rope, fumbling to open the razor, sinking much faster than he had hoped. Ears popped, lungs compressing as he strained to bend while being pulled downward.

The blade proved sharp. Kicking like a dolphin, his feet still bound, he swam with desperate strokes, lungs on fire.

He broke the surface gasping, pleading to the God who didn't exist, that no eyes be watching. That day, his belief changed. The yacht had sped onward with no one caring to see him die, no one except a beautiful young girl named Misha, a princess of Persia, a princess in love with a farm boy from Montana.

For two hours, Jake swam slowly, following the direction of the yacht. Having dropped the razor when swimming up, he spent a long time undoing the rope about his feet.

No sign of land rose anywhere on the endless horizon of blue. The sea was rather calm, but the swells made swimming feel pointless.

"She saw me," he kept repeating, trying to stir hope. He had seen her watching from an upper deck, running off seconds after he broke the surface.

Maybe she'll tell her mother. He fanned at the desperate hope. *But how long can I drift? How long before the sharks come?*

He recalled their time in the wine cask, crammed in close, legs cramping, her breath on his face.

Even if Misha managed to come back, how would she find him—a tiny dot, rising and falling with the swells?

"I'm alive," he said with a measure of satisfaction but then groaned. *Should have just followed the anchor down,* he thought, fear and despair filling his heart.

He shook his head in anger.

"Should have just shot the swine!" He then belted out an angry curse, knowing he couldn't have killed Misha's father, not with her watching. "Even to save my own life. What a fool."

He chuckled for a bit, thinking how he had guessed the man's impotence. Misha was a daughter through marriage, that was now clear enough. Those other young women gave no sons. A sheik without a male heir, only a daughter, not even his own.

"I nailed it," he said with a sardonic chuckle. "Does she know? Didn't seem like it."

Something bumped his leg, jolting his flesh. He kicked about, trying to feel for what loomed beneath, wishing he had the razor. Again, something passed by, long and leathery.

"Come on!" He prayed to his newfound God. "She saw me," he called out. "Please... help her find me."

Something rammed his leg, knocking it hard to one side.

"Misha!" he yelled, fear gripping. "If only..."

Again, something large passed by. He spun about, seeing nothing. "God... please."

INTO THE LIGHT

19

JAKE KICKED HARD, striking something that churned the water beneath. His heart raced as he waited, but nothing more came. For several hours he tread water, the sun slowly melding into the sea. It was a most spectacular display of peachy-orange and soft crimson purples splashed across the sky.

When full darkness came, he shivered, but gave thanks that the shark had wandered on looking for less aggressive prey. Curling into a ball, he rose and fell with the swells, shivering and muttering, longing to say one last goodbye, to say all that burned in his heart.

"I love her," he muttered weakly. "Any guy would," a voice countered. "No, I love *her*. She's so much more than just beautiful."

The image of her holding the knife to her chest made him sick. "Oh, God, she was actually... oh, God."

As the sky lit up with a million stars, he lost track of all time, drifting endlessly, his mind playing every moment of the last two weeks. Scene by scene, he saw her face, her lovely form, the way she moved so... so...

He couldn't find the word, other than he loved watching her, the way she walked and held her head, the way she moved her hands—a delicate, yet strong grace, filled with charm—a pleasure to just watch. More than attractive or beautiful, she was female perfection, a work of the gods, a gift from heaven to the men of earth.

'I believe in you, Yacov. I believe you will find food... for us.' Misha's words came loud and clear as if whispered into his ear. He remembered that moment, how it had thrilled his heart, how he'd treasured those words day after difficult day.

No one believed in him like Misha. Never had he done the things he'd done these past days. Fire and food, the serpent, the men in black, the ordeal with her father, and now, drifting through cold darkness... still longing, yearning to see her one last time.

He closed his eyes, shivering hard in spasms, struggling to hold his legs and stay afloat. "I believe in you, Misha. I believe you will come back for me... for us."

The words were but a whisper, spoken through cold, numb lips. He believed, but also knew he could not last much longer.

In his mind, he spoke his last goodbye. *I kept my promise… protected you… got you back to your father—a real jerk, I'm sorry to say, but…*

He hated himself for holding the gun to her father's head. "That was stupid!" The bitter words went out over the waves, quickly swallowed by the empty darkness.

No wonder she didn't come back. Holding a gun to a future father-in-law. "Father-in-law? Are you completely insane?"

The conversation continued, some spoken into the damp darkness, some spoken to the darkness inside, replaying all the events with commentary exemplifying the noble, brave character of 'Yacov Connor.'

"I didn't touch her," he said toward the starry sky. "Wanted to… I'll admit freely to that. Maybe should've… No! She's a princess, a daughter of Venus. You don't mess around with a girl like that."

He groaned from deep anguish. It wasn't remorse, wasn't pity—it was the darkest sadness—the sadness of a love… forever lost.

"Ah!"

Something bumped his back. Then a large fin struck his leg. Large, for the water had swirled hard as it passed.

Heart now thumping hard, he searched the darkness. He pulled his legs up, clutching them, watching a dorsal fin break the surface, just a little, but enough to show size.

He cursed. "So this is it, huh?"

His heart hammered painfully hard, but a strange peace had come. *I've lived well, kind of.* His lungs were panting fast, but his mind remained calm. *Not very long, but… it's been good.* Scenes of Misha rushed in.

Was worth it… worth it all.

Another bump and swirl.

"Make it fast, you pig!" His angry cry drifted over the waves.

The wind had increased as the night thickened, some waves breaking into spray. A low moan, like blowing on a large glass bottle, drifted through the darkness. The beast beneath made one more pass. Jake yelled with rage.

"Come on!" he shouted. "Just do it! Get it over with!"

Holding his legs tight, he waited in horrid silence, the wind-driven swells lifting him in their arms, dropping him into their depths. For a long, tense time he bobbed in the swells, rising and falling, waiting and praying, muttering the name of Misha.

The sky had darkened, black without a star. In the distance, lightning flashed, like the night they had met, shipwrecked together, lives forever changed. Another flash, closer this time, illuminated the surrounding waves. In the blue light, a large dorsal fin cut the water, straight for him.

"Dear God…" he whispered, closing his eyes.

Another bright flash, followed by a crackling rumble that filled the air above him. It boomed and echoed like from a gun. A bright light flashed, then shone all around. He spun to look about, to find the shark, to fight till the end. Another rumbling crack resounded, the light still burning bright.

Weird lightning, he thought, wondering why the shark hadn't struck.

A distant voice pierced the darkness. Jake tried to see, but the light was so bright.

So this is death, he thought. *Bright light, then it's over.*

Something grabbed him, yanking him out of the dark water into the light. Voices grew louder, making sounds he didn't know. Then his flesh turned to rubber and the light went black.

RESCUE?

20

"JAKE CONNOR," a deep voice said, "from Montana." A wealthy-looking, Middle Eastern man studied the young American, the dark eyes narrowed and thoughtful.

Jake sat dressed in very nice casual-fitting clothes, his belly full from an exquisite breakfast. His host, Aramayis Sevan, rubbed his smooth, defined chin, a slight smile lifting one cheek. The sun broke from a single cloud just moments before as the two men sat on the high deck of a huge yacht, watching the gulls swirl overhead.

"Seventeen days," the man said, "you spent with this one named Misha?"

Jake nodded. For the past two hours, he had told this man his whole story as the sun warmed the deck, as they cruised the open sea with a stretch of land on the far horizon.

"Is she truly that lovely?" the man asked.

"She's beautiful…" Jake's eyes drifted off, his heart saddened, wondering where she might be.

"And wore nothing but silk pajamas?"

"And my t-shirt." *Which did little*, he thought.

"Yet… you did not… dishonor her?"

"No sir, I swear. I vowed to protect her."

"So you did not find her attractive, or sexy, as you Americans say?"

"Attractive?" Jake laughed, thinking back to the day Misha had asked that same question. "If you saw Misha, you would never ask such a question."

"Why?"

"She's a goddess, that's why. A gift from heaven, a woman of such form and beauty to have ever walked the earth till this day. I swear, in all the world, no woman compares to Misha, Princess of Lahar."

He stopped to compose himself, embarrassed at his rambling. "Yes, she is very attractive. I would give my life to see her once more." His voice trailed off as he spoke, pain squeezing his heart.

"And that is the wound?" Aramayis pointed to the jagged red scab on his arm.

"Yeah, vowed to kill the beast."

"Like you tried to kill those men?"

"I wasn't trying to kill them," he said. "Just trying to protect…" He sighed. "I've never done that sort of thing. Not sure it was even real."

"Oh, it was real."

Jake stiffened, gripping his chair. His rescuer, an obviously wealthy man, had up to this point, been a very gracious host. He now seemed to know more than he'd previously revealed.

Jake paled, a cold chill creeping up. "Are you… the uncle?"

The man just stared.

Jake swallowed. "I'm sorry… I did what… was trying to protect Misha…" His mouth felt like chalk.

Silence held the two men as gulls wove back and forth. Jake's gut tightened. This was Torik's father. These guys blew up the cruise ship, murdered Murik the bodyguard.

Oh, God! Jake slumped back, panic rising. It quickly turned to bitterness, an angry bitterness toward God. *Why*, he challenged, *are you toying with me? Is this how you get your kicks?*

In total despair, he let go of everything—all hope, all belief in God, all the stupid dreams of seeing Misha again.

Fate has declared it, he conceded. *I've been marked for death.*

Three times he'd escaped Death's hand only to now meet him here, wearing the face of a wealthy man in casual garb.

"So… you want her too," Jake said in a weak voice.

"Of course!" the man said firmly. "I have sought her for sixteen years."

"Sixteen years?" Jake sat up, stupefied.

The man leaned forward. "Mr. Connor, Misha is my daughter."

With that, a form moved out from behind a tall-backed chair. In flowing silks of vibrant colors, strode the beautiful Misha, Princess of Persia. Blinking back tears, she walked slowly toward Jake. He tried to stand but faltered.

"Misha! What…?"

Wiping her eyes, she came and stood before him. Bejeweled with hair shimmering, her radiance left him breathless.

"How…? You…" He seemed to lose all function.

When she came close, she took his hands in hers, eyes twinkling.

For a time she just studied his face as she'd often done on the island.

Jake stood aghast, unable to respond. He glanced warily to his host, Aramayis, the man who just declared himself her father.

Misha then smiled wide, exhaling a soft sigh. "Am I really a goddess?" she said. "Do my eyes truly look upon Yacov Connor, my noble protector?"

A strange panic rushed Jake's soul. *Is this real? Have I gone insane? Lost in some hallucination, never to return?* Unable to move, he just stood staring at her.

Misha squeezed his hands, eyes glowing. "Thank you,

Yacov," she said softly, "for getting me off Isle of Sunset."

"Is it really you?" he croaked, struggling to speak. "Or am I dreaming?"

She continued to smile up at him, her hair flitting about. "Do I look real?" She squeezed his hands again, drawing him in, but stopped, glancing toward Aramayis.

Completely dumbfounded, Jake blinked, trying to clear a host of tears. Staring into Misha's dark eyes, her face so radiant, he could barely whisper. "I... I only dreamed of seeing you again. I'm... so sorry for... the gun... I just..."

She touched his lips, then took his hand as they sat together on a small couch. Misha's true father watched with a curious eye.

Jake glanced between the two, mouth hanging, heart pulsing way too fast.

"Please tell him, Father," Misha said, speaking the word, 'Father,' with a child-like sweetness. He nodded.

"Fariborz Rahbar and I loved the same woman, but she chose me, of course," he said with a grin. Then his face soured. "But that donkey of a man stole my wife and Misha during the war. She was but a child. For sixteen years her brother Torik and I have searched, always coming close but never able to reclaim them."

He glanced toward the sea, his face set hard.

"We found them that night aboard your ship, but my men were discovered. His baboons were insane, one fool releasing a grenade, exploding fuel tanks. My sorrow is deep. Mercy, oh God."

He wagged his head as in disbelief. "Torik saw her jump but could not follow as he'd been badly wounded. In great agony, he watched her struggle, then finally reach that strange, yellow tub."

Aramayis went on to tell how they searched for days, unable to find the cask until a week later near a small island. They scoured the island with no signs of Misha. Convinced she was not dead, they finally found the 'Isle of Sunset,' but learned that Fariborz also knew.

"It was a race for Misha," he said solemnly.

Jake felt sick. "So… was Torik—?"

"No," Misha said quickly, "he still on crutches." She smiled briefly, gaze distant. "When I see him this morning… I knew him!" She gave a sheepish grin. "How is that… I remember him?" Her smile looked so joyful, so peaceful.

Then seeing the troubled look on Jake's face, she added, "The man you banged with your club, he is okay. Hurts much, but okay."

"And the others," Jake asked.

"Recovering," Aramayis said, "wounded most in their pride."

Her father then told how, after the island incident, they followed Fariborz's yacht and in darkness made a raid, where they rescued Misha and Leyla, her mother.

"She was in a hopeless state," he said, glancing at Misha, who nodded.

"It was strange," she said. "As mother told me whole truth, and I see my true father…" She wiped her eyes.

"All came back, all memories, charging in like horses running fast."

Aramayis watched, his handsome face smiling. "She told Leyla all about you," he continued, "giving the GPS coordinates, so we searched. We followed the currents but saw no hope in finding you. When we did, you had company, a good-sized one salivating with eyes only for you." He chuckled. "Fate brought us just in time."

An elegantly attractive woman stepped onto the deck—Misha's mother. Jake rose and bowed slightly. She nodded.

"Fate provoked by Love," she said, sitting beside her husband, chatting in Farsi for a moment. "I saw your eyes," she said to Jake, her voice smooth, "when you set down the gun. You surrendered yourself, giving your life for my daughter's."

She reached and took her long-lost husband's hand as tears moistened her eyes. "I believe Fate and Love were also watching, watching all of us."

Jake just stared, trying to steady his trembling hands. His thoughts were still jumbled in a state of bewilderment, still questioning the day's reality.

A young girl came, bringing sliced fruit and sweet cakes, with coffee poured in tiny cups. Jake listened as the others talked in a mix of English and Farsi, eating and sipping, motioning for him to join in.

He heard the name Murik, Misha's old bodyguard. She caught his inquisitive eye. "Mother just saying he was murdered by Fariborz. Fit of angry that Murik didn't find me." She shook her head. "So sad. A good man."

Jake too wagged his head. It was all too surreal, so unbelievable. He kept wondering if he had died and this was some form of heaven. He watched Misha, her beauty once again captivating every fiber of his soul. Knowing this may be his last chance, he boldly stared, hoping to memorize her movements, her smiling laughter, the waves of her long black hair floating freely about her face. He watched her eat, her enchanting eyes passing intimate glances his way.

No… this can't be real!

She smiled at him, flinging her hair back. Then rested her hand on his.

"Eat some fruit, Yacov. It is… okay."

A cool wariness kept all joy at bay, his mind and heart unable to trust this strange new reality.

How can this be real? he kept asking. Whether real or not, he still had one burning question troubling his heart.

Clearing his throat, he prepared his words carefully. "I know I'm an infidel," he said, bringing their vibrant conversation to an abrupt halt, "but I need to ask something. Sorry, but… I really… well… is there any way on earth… or heaven, if that's where we are, that I can somehow… keep in contact with… your daughter… Misha?"

He quickly bowed his head, grimacing with eyes tight, fearing he had asked too much. When only silence followed, he slumped back with a groan.

LOVE AND FATE
21

AS THE DREADFUL SILENCE continued, Jake opened his mouth to apologize, to beg forgiveness for being so rude. But Misha's mother spoke first.

"I believe Love has given Fate a firm poke." She took her husband's hand. "You wish to stay in contact with Misha?"

Jake looked up, nodding like a boy just offered ice cream.

"Of course," Leyla continued. She paused, watching Jake who looked expectantly at her. "There is a way to see her... every day."

Jake sat up, wondering if he'd heard right.

"She's given us no choice," Aramayis said rather bluntly. "We have talked long, and now request of you one essential requirement."

Jake held his breath. He glanced to Misha, who just sat with a smug grin. Her father then took a long hard look at Jake.

"Today's world has changed," he said. "Noble men, those with strong hearts, are not confined to families of wealth and stature, nor to country or belief. So we have consented… asking only one stipulation."

"That I become… Muslim?" Jake asked, the words sounding strange.

Both parents drew back while Misha giggled.

"No," said Aramayis, a bit startled, "we're Armenian. Christian Armenians for generations." He then cocked his head, eyes squinting. "Do you wish to become Muslim?"

"No! I just thought…"

Leyla reached over and took Jake's hand. "We ask," she began, leaning close, "that you never take her from us. That is all. And that you promise to protect and love her as you have so demonstrated. Can you promise that?"

Jake sat breathless, blond head slowly wagging.

A moment passed.

Misha drew a deep breath, her astonished stare intense.

"I'm sorry," Jake finally said, giving Misha a look of exasperation.

She exhaled sharply. "What! You cannot promise this?" Her voice rose to a tense squeak.

"I'm sorry," Jake said again, "but I'm totally confused. What is going on here? You're not Muslim? And you want me to…do what?" His confused gaze went from Misha to Mother, to Father, and back again.

A second of silence passed, then both parents chuckled.

"Jake Connor," Leyla finally said, "if you could have anything in this world, what do you desire?"

Jake shook his head. "I don't want any reward. I owe you everything. You saved my life. I appreciate the offer, but…" He glanced at Misha. "All I'm asking is if I can visit, you know, see her sometime. If not, I understand, but…" Once again he felt stupid, still wondering if any of this were real.

Misha's father became stern. "I like you, Jake. But you must answer me now. If you could ask me for one thing, what would it be?"

Struggling to understand, Jake panicked. "As I said, sir, I don't expect anything. You've been very kind to me. I don't need or want anything." He shot a troubled glance to Misha, heart pounding.

She glared at him, her chest rising and falling rapidly. He knew that look.

"All I want," Jake suddenly declared. "If I can speak freely. I wish… I could spend the rest of my life with your daughter… Misha. That's what I *really* want."

At this, Misha sank back, exhaling a long, sweet sigh. Aramayis nodded, his gaze still locked on Jake. Then he slowly stood and taking Leyla's hand, helped her stand. Misha followed suit as Aramayis nodded to Jake. He joined them, standing rather warily. Leyla put her arm around her husband, who then took a deep breath. He was a tall, sturdy man with strong features. He faced Jake for a moment, looking hard into the young man's eyes.

"Then it shall be," he finally said. Grasping Jake's right hand, he gently took Misha's left. Once again, he studied the young man's face. "Do you, Jake Connor," he said in a very solemn tone, "promise before me her father, before God her creator, before Leyla her faithful mother, to protect and love Misha with all your strength and soul?"

Still lost in bewilderment, Jake looked down at the circle of hands now joined by Leyla. His brain had gone completely numb. Misha nudged him with a little kick.

As if jolted awake, he sputtered, "P-promise?"

Then the lights came on. "Yes! Yes, I promise to battle heaven and earth for her… if you're asking what I think you're asking. Are you asking…?"

He didn't wait, his face flushing bold.

"I will love her more and more each day if you're giving me that chance. Are you… am I reading this right?" He looked back and forth between them, then to Misha for help.

Aramayis and Leyla just watched with growing wonder. Then Aramayis spoke.

"And further," he said, pausing to once more study Jake, "can you promise to never take her from us, like to Montana, but live with us for the rest of our days?"

Jake tried to answer, but his throat had choked, eyes awash with tears. Nodding his head profusely, he stammered out, "Are you... offering your daughter... Misha... in marriage... to *me*?"

"I've little choice," Aramayis said. "So, young man, what is your answer? If I entrust my daughter, will you consent to live with us?"

Still befuddled, Jake stood processing. *A dream! Has to be a dream. I'm still in the water... unconscious... No, it's real!*

Turning to look at Misha, he then dropped to one knee. "Misha, goddess of all that is graceful and full of beauty, the only woman I admire and adore with all my heart and soul, if you would consider this lowly man to be your eternal mate, then with joy beyond description I humbly ask your hand in marriage, to give me the chance to love you every moment we live together."

He paused to catch his breath, stunned at his own words, words he'd practiced while drifting hopeless in the sea, words he only spoke in dreamy visions with heart-sick longing.

"Misha, princess of all that is true and lovely, would you accept my promise of protection and love? Will you be... my wife?"

Misha, in all her grace and beauty, pressed her lips tight, eyes beaming, tears slowly trailing her cheeks. She too could only nod, a vigorous, passionate nod. Finally, her voice managed a whispered reply.

"Yes, Yacov Connor, I so want to be your wife."

Jake stood, glancing at Misha's father, who gave a

consenting nod. Before he'd realized what had just happened, Misha flung her arms around his middle, her face pressed to his chest.

He glanced up into a beautiful sky—clouds painted by the morning sun rose high, gulls sailed on the warm wind, a cerulean sea lay calm all about them. "Thank you," he whispered, "beyond all imagining… so don't deserve this… thank you!"

DAWN
22

JAKE OPENED HIS EYES. The rocky ceiling reflected the morning's light with a reddish glow. He turned, feeling the grass mat beneath him.

No! Nooo…!

Deep sorrow crushed his soul, tears flooding his eyes. "Nooo!" he moaned. "No, no, no…"

A lovely form stirred close beside him. Dressed in soft silks, with golden thread woven through her braid, lay the Princess of Persia.

Misha rolled over with a moan, her arm flopping over Jake's naked chest. Blinking into the sun's warm light, she brushed her long fingers over his jaw. Jake saw the rings on her fingers, rings he had given her, rings that bore his promise.

"Good morning, Khabe delam," she said with eyes twinkling, her voice a bit husky. "You are indeed my heart's dream."

Then all came back in full glory as joy gushed his soul. He propped on an elbow, looking out over the glistening sea, jubilant relief lifting his face. They were still on their honeymoon. It had been Misha's desire to return to the Isle of Sunset and spend a night inside the cave.

'We must, Yakov… for us,' she had said.

Jake thought back to last night. As the setting westward sun painted the eastern sky, the two lovers had lain together on their grass mats in the small cave overlooking the sea. The mats that once lay apart, separated by an ever-burning fire, now lay side-by-side, a fire still burning, that ancient fire of passion fueled by true love.

"For us…" Jake whispered, smiling down on his young bride. Then, with overwhelming joy, he lay back and gently kissed his beautiful Misha, Princess of Persia.

ABOUT THE AUTHOR

Lew has four adult children, a growing number of grandchildren, and has been happily married to one amazing woman for the past forty years.

He and his family spent six years in Northern Asia helping impoverished schools while teaching English. "Often, I'd be the first 'white man' these mountainous areas had ever seen." After receiving his M.A. in the Philippines, he returned to pastor a church in his home state of Minnesota.

"I have always loved writing, as I believe we were meant to be creative—to then share our talent for others to enjoy. Many underestimate their natural gifts, fearing failure or criticism. I encourage you to explore those riches—to dream big, to work hard, and never give up."

For more about Lew Anderson and his writing, you're welcome to visit *www.lewanderson.com*

www.ingramcontent.com/pod-product-compliance
Lightning Source LLC
Chambersburg PA
CBHW031027190726
48286CB00003BA/1056